MICHAEL

VICTORIAN VILLAINY

A COLLECTION OF MORIARTY STORIES

Complete and Unabridged

LINFORD
Leicester

First published in Great Britain

First Linford Edition
published 2013

A catalogue record for this book is available
from the British Library.

ISBN 978–1–4448–1545–0

Published by
F. A. Thorpe (Publishing)
Anstey, Leicestershire

Set by Words & Graphics Ltd.
Anstey, Leicestershire
Printed and bound in Great Britain by
T. J. International Ltd., Padstow, Cornwall

This book is printed on acid-free paper

1

Years Ago and in a Different Place

My name is Professor James Clovis Moriarty, Ph.D., F.R.A.S. You may have heard of me. I have been the author of a number of well-regarded scientific monographs and journal articles over the past few decades, including a treatise on the Binomial Theorem, and a monograph titled 'The Dynamics of an Asteroid,' which was well received in scientific circles both in Great Britain and on the continent. My recent paper in the *British Astronomical Journal*, 'Observations on the July 1889 Eclipse of Mercury with Some Speculations Concerning the Effect of Gravity on Light Waves,' has occasioned some comment among those few who could understand its implications.

But I fear that if you know my name, it is, in all probability, not through any of my published scientific papers. Further, my current, shall I say, notoriety, was not of my own doing and most assuredly not by my choice. I am by nature a retiring, some would have it secretive, person.

Over the past few years narratives from the memoirs of a certain Dr. John Watson concerning that jackanapes who calls himself a 'consulting detective,' Mr. Sherlock Holmes, have been appearing in the *Strand* magazine and elsewhere with increasing frequency and have attained, to my mind, a most unwarranted popularity. Students of the 'higher criticism,' as those insufferable pedants who devote their lives to picking over minuscule details of Dr. Watson's stories call their ridiculous avocation, have analyzed Watson's rather pedestrian prose with the avid attention gourmands pay to mounds of goose-liver pâté. They extract hidden meanings from every word, and extrapolate facts not in evidence from every paragraph. Which leads them unfailingly to conclusions even more specious than those in which Holmes himself indulges.

Entirely too much of this misdirected musing concerns me and my relationship with the self-anointed master detective. Amateur detection enthusiasts have wasted much time and energy in speculation as to how Sherlock Holmes and I first met, and just what caused the usually unflappable Holmes to describe me as 'the Napoleon of crime' without supplying the slightest evidence to support this blatant canard.

I propose to tell that story now, both to satisfy this misplaced curiosity and to put an end to the various speculations which have appeared in certain privately-circulated monographs. To set the record straight: Holmes and I are *not* related; I have *not* had improper relations with any of his female relatives; I did *not* steal his childhood inamorata away from him. Neither did he, to the best of my knowledge, perform any of these services for me or anyone in my family.

In any case, I assure you that I will no longer take such accusations lightly. Privately distributed though these monographs may be, their authors will have to answer for them in a court of law if this continues.

Shortly before that ridiculous episode

at the Reichenbach Falls, Holmes had the temerity to describe me to his befuddled amanuensis as 'organizer of half that is evil and nearly all that is undetected in this great city.' (By which he meant London, of course.) What crimes I had supposedly committed he was curiously silent about. Watson did not ask for specifics, and none were offered. The good doctor took Holmes's unsupported word for this insupportable insult. Had Holmes not chosen to disappear for three years after his foul accusation, I most assuredly would have had him in the dock for slander.

And then, when Holmes returned from his extended vacation, during which time he did not have the kindness, the decency, to pass on one word that would let his dear companion know that he was not dead, he gave an account of our 'struggle' at the falls that any child of nine would have recognized as a complete work of fiction — but it fooled Watson.

The truth about the Reichenbach incident — but no, that is not for this narrative. Just permit me a brief pause, the merest aside in this chronicle before I go on, so that I may draw your attention to some of the details of that story that should have alerted the merest tyro to the fact that he was being diddled — but that Watson swallowed whole.

In the narrative that he published under the name 'The Final Problem,' Watson relates that Holmes appeared in his consulting room one day in April of 1891 and told him that he was being threatened by Professor Moriarty — myself — and that he had already been attacked twice that day by my agents and expected to be attacked again, probably by a man using an air-rifle. If that were so, was it not thoughtful of him to go to the residence of his close friend and thus place him, also, in deadly peril?

At that meeting Holmes declares that in three days he will be able to place 'the Professor, with all the principal members of his gang,' in the hands of the police. Why wait? Holmes gives no coherent reason. But until then, Holmes avers, he is in grave danger. Well now! If this were so, would not Scotland Yard gladly have given Holmes a room, nay a suite of rooms, in the hotel of his choosing — or in the Yard itself — to keep him safe for the next three days? But Holmes says that nothing will do but that he must flee the country, and once again Watson believes him. Is not unquestioning friendship a wonderful thing?

Holmes then arranges for Watson to join him in this supposedly hasty flight. They meet at Victoria Station the next morning, where Watson has trouble recognizing Holmes, who has disguised himself as a 'venerable Italian priest,' presumably to fool pursuers. This assumes that Holmes's enemies can recognize the great detective, but have no idea what his good friend Dr. Watson, who wears no disguise, who indeed is congenitally incapable of disguise, looks like.

Again note that after a six-month absence, during which Holmes and I — but no, it is not my secret to tell. At any rate, six months after I was assumed to be dead I returned to my home on Russell Square and went about my business as usual, and Watson affected not to notice.

After all, Holmes had killed me, and that was good enough for Watson.

I could go on. Indeed, it is with remarkable restraint that I do not. To describe me as a master criminal is actionable; and then to compound matters by making me out to be such a bungler as to be fooled by Holmes's juvenile antics is quite intolerable. It should be clear to all that the events leading up to that day at Reichenbach Falls, if they occurred as described, were designed by Holmes to fool his amiable companion, and not 'the Napoleon of crime.'

But I have digressed enough. In this brief paper I will describe how the relationship between Holmes and myself came to be, and perhaps supply some insight into how and why Holmes developed an entirely unwarranted antagonism toward me that has lasted these many years.

I first met Sherlock Holmes in the early 1870s — I shall be no more precise than that. At the time I was a senior lecturer in mathematics at, I shall call it, 'Queens

College,' one of the six venerable colleges making up a small inland university which I shall call 'Wexleigh' to preserve the anonymity of the events I am about to describe. I shall also alter the names of the persons who figure in this episode, save only those of Holmes and myself; as those who were involved surely have no desire to be reminded of the episode or pestered by the press for more details. You may, of course, apply to Holmes for the true names of these people, although I imagine that he will be no more forthcoming than I.

Let me also point out that memories are not entirely reliable recorders of events. Over time they convolute, they conflate, they manufacture, and they discard, until what remains may bear only a passing resemblance to the original event. So if you happen to be one of the people whose lives crossed those of Holmes and myself at 'Queens' at this time, and your memory of some of the details of these events differs from mine, I assure you that in all probability we are both wrong.

Wexleigh University was of respectable antiquity, with respectable ecclesiastical underpinnings. Most of the dons at Queens were churchmen of one description or another. Latin and Greek were still considered the foundations upon which an education should be constructed. The 'modern' side of the university had come into existence a mere decade before, and the Classics dons still looked with mixed amazement and scorn at the Science instructors and the courses offered, which they insisted on describing as 'Stinks and Bangs.'

Holmes was an underclassman at the time. His presence had provoked a certain amount of interest among the faculty, many of whom remembered his brother Mycroft, who had attended the university some six years previously. Mycroft had spent most of his three years at Queens in his room, coming out only for meals and to gather armfuls of books from the library and retreat back to his room. When he did appear in the lecture hall it would often be to correct the instructor on some error of fact or pedagogy that had lain unnoticed, sometimes for years, in one of his lectures. Mycroft had departed the university without completing the requirements for a degree, stating with some justification that he had received all the institution had to offer, and he saw no point in remaining.

Holmes had few friends among his fellow underclassmen and seemed to prefer it that way. His interests were varied but transient, as he dipped first into one field of study and then another, trying to find something that stimulated him sufficiently for him to make it his life's work; something to which he could apply his powerful intellect and his capacity for close and accurate observation, which was even then apparent, if not fully developed.

An odd sort of amity soon grew between myself and this intense young man. On looking back I would describe it as a cerebral bond, based mostly on the shared snobbery of the highly intelligent against those whom they deem as their intellectual inferiors. I confess to that weakness in my youth, and my only defense against a charge of hubris is that those whom we went out of our way to ignore were just as anxious to avoid us.

The incident I am about to relate occurred in the Fall, shortly after Holmes returned to begin his second year. A new don joined the college, occupying the newly-created chair of Moral Philosophy, a chair which had been endowed by a midlands mill owner who made it a practice to employ as many children under twelve in his mills as his agents could sweep up off the streets. Thus, I suppose, his interest in Moral Philosophy.

The new man's name was — well, for the purposes of this tale let us call him Professor Charles Maples. He was, I would judge, in his mid forties; a stout, sharp-nosed, myopic, amiable man who strutted and bobbed slightly when he walked. His voice was high and intense, and his mannerisms were complex. His speech was accompanied by elaborate hand motions, as though he would mold the air into a semblance of what he was describing. When one saw him crossing the quad in the distance, with his gray

11

master of arts gown flapping about him, waving the mahogany walking-stick with the brass duck's-head handle that he was never without, and gesticulating to the empty air, he resembled nothing so much as a corpulent king pigeon.

Moral Philosophy was a fit subject for Maples. No one could say exactly what it encompassed, and so he was free to speak on whatever caught his interest at the moment. And his interests seemed to be of the moment: he took intellectual nourishment from whatever flower of knowledge seemed brightest to him in the morning, and had tired of it ere night drew nigh. Excuse the vaguely poetic turn of phrase; speaking of Maples seems to bring that out in one.

I do not mean to suggest the Maples was intellectually inferior; far from it. He had a piercing intellect, an incisive clarity of expression, and a sarcastic wit that occasionally broke through his mild façade. Maples spoke on the Greek and Roman concept of manliness, and made one regret that we lived in these decadent times. He lectured on the nineteenth century penchant for substituting a surface prudery for morality, and left his students with a vivid image of unnamed immorality seething and billowing not very far beneath the surface. He spoke on this and that and created in his students an abiding enthusiasm for this, and an unremitting loathing for that.

There was still an unspoken presumption about the college that celibacy was the proper model for the students, and so only the unmarried, and presumably celibate, dons were lodged in one or another of the various buildings within the college walls. Those few with wives found housing around town where they could, preferably a respectable distance from the university. Maples was numbered among the domestic ones, and he and his wife Andrea had taken a house with fairly extensive grounds on Barleymore Road not far from the college, which they shared with Andrea's sister Lucinda Moys and a physical education instructor named Crisboy, who, choosing to live away from the college for reasons of his own, rented a pair of rooms on the top floor. There was a small guest house at the far end of the property which was untenanted. The owner of the property, who had moved to Glasgow some years previously, kept it for his own use on his occasional visits to town. The Maples employed a cook and a maid, both of whom were day help, sleeping in their own homes at night.

Andrea was a fine-looking woman who appeared to be fearlessly approaching thirty, with intelligent brown eyes set in a broad face and a head of thick, brown hair, which fell down her back to somewhere below her waist when she didn't have it tied up in a sort of oversized bun circling her head. She was of a solid appearance and decisive character.

Her sister, 'Lucy' to all who knew her, was somewhat younger and more ethereal in nature. She was a slim, golden-haired creature of mercurial moods: usually bright and confident and more than capable of handling anything the mean old world could throw at her, but on occasion dark and sullen and angry at the rest of the world for not measuring up to her standards. When one of her moods overtook her, she retired to her room and refused to see anyone until it passed, which for some reason the young men of the college found intensely romantic. She had an intent manner of gazing at you while you conversed, as though your words were the only things of importance in the world at that instant, and she felt privileged to be listening. This caused several of the underclassmen to fall instantly in love with her, as she was perhaps the first person, certainly the first woman aside from their mothers, who had ever paid serious attention to anything they said.

One of the underclassmen who was attracted by Miss Lucy's obvious charms was Mr. Sherlock Holmes. She gazed at him wide-eyed while he spoke earnestly, as young men speak, of things that I'm sure must have interested her not in the least. Was it perhaps Holmes himself who interested the pert young lady? I certainly hoped so, for his sake. Holmes had no sisters, and a man who grows up without sisters has few defenses against those wiles, those innocent wiles of body, speech and motion, with which nature has provided young females in its blind desire to propagate the species.

I was not a close observer of the amorous affairs of Lucy Moys, but as far as I could see she treated all her suitors the same; neither encouraging them nor discouraging them, but enjoying their company and keeping them at a great enough distance, both physically and emotionally, to satisfy the most demanding duenna. She seemed to me to find all her young gentlemen vaguely amusing, regarding them with the sort of detachment one finds in the heroines of Oscar Wilde's plays, to use a modern simile.

Professor Maples took the *in loco parentis* role of the teacher a bit further than most of the faculty, and certainly further than I would have cared to, befriending his students, and for that matter any students who desired to be befriended, earnestly, sincerely and kindly. But then he seemed to truly care about the needs and welfare of the young men of Wexleigh. Personally I felt that attempting to educate most of them in class and at tutorials was quite enough. For the most part they cared for nothing but sports, except for those who cared for nothing but religion, and were content to allow the sciences and mathematics to remain dark mysteries.

Maples and his wife had 'at home' afternoon teas twice a month, the second and fourth Tuesdays, and quite soon these events became very popular with the students. His sister-in-law, who was invariably present, was certainly part of the reason, as was the supply of tea-cakes, scones, fruit tarts, and other assorted edibles. I attended several of these, and was soon struck by an indefinable feeling that something was not what it seemed. I say 'indefinable' because I could not put my finger on just what it was that puzzled me about the events. I did not attach too much importance to it at the time. It was only later that it seemed significant. I will try to give you a word picture of the last of these events that I attended; the last one, as it happens, before the tragedy.

It was Holmes who suggested that we attend Professor Maples's tea that day. I had been trying to impress upon him a rudimentary understanding of the calculus, and he had demanded of me an example of some situation in which such knowledge might be of use. I outlined three problems, one from astronomy, involving the search for the planet Vulcan, said to lie inside the orbit of Mercury; one from physics, relating to determining magnetic lines of force when an electric current is applied; and one based on some thoughts of my own regarding Professor Malthus's notions on population control.

Holmes waved them all aside. 'Yes, I am sure they are very interesting in their own way,' he said, 'but, frankly, they do not concern me. It does not matter to me whether the Earth goes around the Sun or the Sun goes around the Earth, as long as whichever does whatever keeps on doing it reliably.'

'You have no intellectual curiosity regarding the world around you?' I asked in some surprise.

'On the contrary,' Holmes averred. 'I have an immense curiosity, but I have no more interest in the Binomial Theorem than it has in me. I feel that I must confine my curiosity to those subjects that will be of some use to me in the future. There is so much to learn on the path I have chosen that I fear that I dare not venture very far along side roads.'

'Ah!' I said. 'I was not aware that you had started down your chosen road, or indeed that you had chosen a road down which to tread.'

Holmes and I were sitting in an otherwise unoccupied lecture hall, and at my words he rose and began pacing restlessly about the front of the room. 'I wouldn't say that I have chosen the road, exactly,' he said, 'to continue with this, I suppose, inescapable metaphor. But I have an idea of the direction in which I wish to travel — ' He made a point of his right forefinger and thrust it forcefully in front of him. ' — and I feel I must carefully limit my steps to paths that go in that direction.'

'Is it that pile of erasers or the

wastebasket at the end of the room at which you hope to arrive?' I asked, and then quickly raised a conciliatory hand. 'No, no, I take it back. I'm glad you have formulated a goal in life, even if it doesn't include the calculus. What is the direction of this city on a hill toward which you strive?'

Holmes glowered at me for a moment and then looked thoughtful. 'It's still slightly vague,' he told me. 'I can see it in outline only. A man — ' He gathered his ideas. 'A man should strive to do something larger than himself. To cure disease, or eradicate hunger or poverty or crime.'

'Ah!' I said. 'Noble thoughts.' I fancied that I could hear the lovely voice of Miss Lucy earnestly saying that, or something similar, to Holmes within the week. When a man is suddenly struck by noble ambitions it is usually a woman who does the striking. But I thought it would be wiser not to mention this deduction, which, at any rate, was rather tentative and not based on any hard evidence.

'It's Professor Maples' afternoon tea

day today,' Holmes commented. 'And I had thought of going.'

'Why so it is,' I said. 'And so we should. And, in one last effort to interest you in the sort of detail for which you find no immediate utility, I call to your attention the shape of Lucinda Moys' ear. Considered properly, it presents an interesting question. You should have an opportunity to observe it, perhaps even fairly closely, this afternoon.'

'Which ear?'

'Either will do.'

'What's the matter with Miss Lucy's ear?' Holmes demanded.

'Why, nothing. It's a delightful ear. Well formed. Flat, rather oblate lobes. I've never seen another quite like it. Very attractive, if it comes to that.'

'All right, then,' Holmes said.

I closed the few books I had been using and put them in my book sack. 'I hereby renounce any future attempt to teach you higher mathematics,' I told him. 'I propose we adjourn and head toward the professor's house and his tea-cakes.'

And so we did.

The Maples' event was from three in the afternoon until six in the evening, although some arrived a bit earlier, and some I believe stayed quite a bit later. The weather was surprisingly mild for mid October, and Holmes and I arrived around half past three that day to find the professor and his household and their dozen or so guests scattered about the lawn behind the house in predictable clumps. The vice-chancellor of the university was present, relaxing in a lawn chair with a cup of tea and a plate of scones. Classical Greece was represented by Dean Herbert McCuthers, an elderly man of intense sobriety and respectability, who was at that moment rolling up his trouser legs preparatory to wading in the small artificial pond with Andrea Maples, who had removed her shoes and hoisted her skirts in a delicate balance between wet clothing and propriety.

Crisboy, the physical education instructor who roomed with the Maples, a large, muscular, and pugnacious-looking man in his late twenties, was standing in one corner of the lawn with a games coach named Faulting; a young man with the build and general appearance of one of the lithe athletes depicted by ancient Greek statuary, if you can picture a young Greek athlete clad in baggy gray flannels. The comparison was one that Faulting was well aware of, judging by his practice of posing heroically whenever he thought anyone was looking at him.

The pair of them were standing near the house, swinging athletic clubs with muscular wild abandon, and discussing the finer details of last Saturday's football match, surrounded by a bevy of admiring underclassmen. There are those students at every university who are more interested in games than education. They spend years afterward talking about this or that cricket match against their mortal foes at the next school over, or some particularly eventful football game. It never seems to bother them, or perhaps even occur to them, that they are engaged in pursuits at which a suitably trained three-year-old chimpanzee or orangutan could best them. And, for some reason that eludes me, these men are allowed to vote and to breed. But, once again, I digress.

Maples was walking magisterially across the lawn, his gray master's gown billowing about his fundament, his hands clasped behind him holding his walking-stick, which jutted out to his rear like a tail, followed by a gaggle of young gentlemen in their dark brown scholars' gowns, with their mortarboards tucked under their arms, most of them giving their professor the subtle homage of imitating his walk and his posture. 'The ideal of the university,' Maples was saying in a voice that would brook no dispute, obviously warming up to his theme, 'is the Aristotelian *stadium* as filtered through the medieval monastic schools.'

He nodded to me as he reached me, and then wheeled about and headed back whence he had come, embroidering on his theme. 'Those students who hungered for something more than a religious education, who perhaps wanted to learn the law, or what there was of medicine, headed toward the larger cities, where

24

savants fit to instruct them could be found. Paris, Bologna, York, London; here the students gathered, often traveling from city to city in search of just the right teacher. After a century or two the instruction became formalized, and the schools came into official existence, receiving charters from the local monarch, and perhaps from the pope.'

Maples suddenly froze in mid-step and wheeled around to face his entourage. 'But make no mistake!' he enjoined them, waving his cane pointedly in front him, its duck-faced head point first at one student and then another, 'a university is not made up of its buildings, its colleges, its lecture halls, or its playing fields. No, not even its playing fields. A university is made up of the people — teachers and students — that come together in its name. *Universitas scholarium*, is how the charters read, providing for a, shall I say guild, of students. Or, as in the case of the University of Paris, a *universitas magistrorum*, a guild of teachers. So we are co-equal, you and I. Tuck your shirt more firmly into your trousers, Mr. Pomfrit, you are becoming all disassembled.'

He turned and continued his journey across the greensward, his voice fading with distance. His students, no doubt impressed with their new-found equality, trotted along behind him.

Lucy Moys glided onto the lawn just then, coming through the French doors at the back of the house, bringing a fresh platter of pastries to the parasol-covered table. Behind her trotted the maid, bringing a pitcher full of steaming hot water to refill the teapot. Sherlock Holmes left my side and wandered casually across the lawn, contriving to arrive by Miss Lucy's side just in time to help her distribute the pastries about the table. Whether he took any special interest in her ear, I could not observe.

I acquired a cup of tea and a slice of tea-cake and assumed my accustomed role as an observer of phenomena. This has been my natural inclination for years, and I have enhanced whatever ability I began with by a conscious effort to accurately take note of what I see. I had practiced this for long enough, even then, that it had become second nature to me. I could not sit opposite a man on a railway car without, for example, noticing by his watch-fob that he was a Rosicrucian, let us say, and by the wear-marks on his left cuff that he was a note-cashier or an order clerk. A smudge of ink on his right thumb would favor the note-cashier hypothesis, while the state of his boots might show that he had not been at work that day. The note-case that he kept clutched to his body might indicate that he was transferring notes to a branch bank, or possibly that he was absconding with the bank's funds. And so on. I go into this only to show that my observations were not made in anticipation of tragedy, but were merely the result of my fixed habit.

I walked about the lawn for the next hour or so, stopping here and there to nod hello to this student or that professor. I lingered at the edge of this group, and listened for a while to a spirited critique of Wilkie Collin's recent novel, 'The Moonstone,' and how it represented an entirely new sort of fiction. I paused by that cluster to hear a young man earnestly explicating on the good works being done by Mr. William Booth and his Christian Revival Association in the slums of our larger cities. I have always distrusted earnest, pious, loud young men. If they are sincere, they're insufferable. If they are not sincere, they're dangerous.

I observed Andrea Maples, who had dried her feet and lowered her skirts, take a platter of pastries and wander around the lawn, offering a cruller here and a tea-cake there, whispering intimate comments to accompany the pastry. Mrs. Maples had a gift for instant intimacy, for creating the illusion that you and she shared wonderful, if unimportant, secrets. She sidled by Crisboy, who was now busy leading five or six of his athletic proteges in doing push-ups, and whispered something to young Faulting, the games coach, and he laughed. And then she was up on her tip-toes whispering some more. After perhaps a minute, which is a long time to be whispering, she danced a few steps back and paused, and Faulting blushed.

Blushing has quite gone out of fashion now, but it was quite the thing for both men and women back in the seventies. Although how something that is believed to be an involuntary physiological reaction can be either in or out of fashion demands more study by Dr. Freud and his fellow psycho-analysts.

Crisboy gathered himself and leaped to his feet. 'Stay on your own side of the street!' he yapped at Andrea Maples, which startled both her and the young gamesmen, two of whom rolled over and stared up at the scene, while the other three or four continued doing push-ups at a frantic pace, as though there was nothing remarkable happening above them. After a second Mrs. Maples laughed and thrust the plate of pastries out at him.

Professor Maples turned to stare at the little group some twenty feet away from him and his hands tightened around his walking stick. Although he strove to remain calm, he was clearly in the grip of some powerful emotion for a few seconds before he regained control. 'Now, now, my dear,' he called across the lawn. 'Let us not incite the athletes.'

Andrea skipped over to him and leaned over to whisper in his ear. As she was facing me this time, and I had practiced lip-reading for some years, I could make out what she said: 'Perhaps I'll do you a favor, my dear,' she whispered. His reply was not visible to me.

A few minutes later my wanderings took me over to where Sherlock Holmes was sitting by himself on one of the canvas chairs near the French windows looking disconsolate. 'Well,' I said, looking around, 'and where is Miss Lucy?'

'She suddenly discovered that she had a sick headache and needed to go lie down. Presumably she has gone to lie down,' he told me.

'I see,' I said. 'Leaving you to suffer alone among the multitude.'

'I'm afraid it must have been something I said,' Holmes confided to me.

'Really? What did you say?'

'I'm not sure. I was speaking about — well . . . ' Holmes looked embarrassed, a look I had never seen him encompass before, nor have I seen it since.

'Hopes and dreams,' I suggested.

'Something of that nature,' he agreed. 'Why is it that words that sound so — important — when one is speaking to a young lady with whom one is on close terms, would sound ridiculous when spoken to the world at large? That is, you understand, Mr. Moriarty, a rhetorical question.'

'I do understand,' I told him. 'Shall we return to the college?'

And so we did.

The next afternoon found me in the commons room sitting in my usual chair beneath the oil painting of Sir James Walsingham, the first chancellor of Queens College, receiving the keys to the college from Queen Elizabeth. I was dividing my attention between my cup of coffee and a letter from the reverend Charles Dodgson, a fellow mathematician who was then at Oxford, in which he put forth some of his ideas concerning what we might call the mathematical constraints of logical constructions. My solitude was interrupted by Dean McCuthers, who toddled over, cup of tea in hand, looking even older than usual, and dropped into the chair next to me. 'Afternoon, Moriarty,' he breathed. 'Isn't it dreadful?'

I put the letter aside. 'Isn't what dreadful?' I asked him. 'The day? The war news? Huxley's Theory of Biogenesis? Perhaps you're referring to the coffee — it is rather dreadful today.'

McCuthers shook his head sadly. 'Would that I could take the news so lightly,' he said. 'I am always so aware, so sadly aware, of John Donne's admonishment.'

'I thought Donne had done with admonishing for these past two hundred years or so,' I said.

But there was no stopping McCuthers. He was determined to quote Donne, and quote he did: ''Any man's death diminishes me, because I am involved in Mankind,'' he went on, ignoring my comment. ''And therefore never send to know for whom the bell tolls; it tolls for thee.''

I forbore from mentioning that the

dean, a solitary man who spent most of his waking hours pondering over literature written over two thousand years before he was born, was probably less involved in mankind than any man I had ever known. 'I see,' I said. 'The bell has tolled for someone?'

'And murder makes it so much worse,' McCuthers continued. 'As Lucretius puts it — '

'Who was murdered?' I asked firmly, cutting through his tour of the classics.

'Eh? You mean you don't know? Oh, dear me. This will come as something of a shock, then. It's that Professor Maples — '

'Someone has murdered Maples?'

'No, no. My thought was unfinished. Professor Maples has been arrested. His wife — Andrea — Mrs. Maples — has been murdered.'

I was, I will admit it, bemused. You may substitute a stronger term if you like. I tried to get some more details from McCuthers, but the dean's involvement with the facts had not gone beyond the murder and the arrest. I finished my coffee and went off in search of more information.

Murder is a sensational crime that evokes a formidable amount of interest, even among the staid and unworldly dons of Queens College. And a murder *in mediis rebus*, or perhaps better, *in mediis universitatibus*; one that actually occurs among said staid dons, will intrude on the contemplations of even the most unworldly. The story, which spread rapidly through the college, was this:

A quartet of bicyclists, underclassmen from St. Simon's College, set out together at dawn three days a week, rain or shine, to get an hour or two's cycling in before breakfast. This morning, undeterred by the chill drizzle that had begun during the night, they went out along Barleymore Road as usual. At about eight o'clock, or shortly after, they happened to stop at the front steps to the small cottage on Professor Maples' property. One of the bicycles had thrown a shoe, or something of the sort, and they had paused to repair the damage. The chain-operated bicycle had been in existence for only a few years back then, and was prone to a variety of malfunctions. I understand that bicyclists, even today, find it useful to carry about a complete set of tools in order to be prepared for the inevitable mishap.

One of the party, who was sitting on the cottage steps with his back up against the door, as much out of the rain as he could manage, indulging in a pipeful of Latakia while the damaged machine was being repaired, felt something sticky under his hand. He looked, and discovered a widening stain coming out from under the door. Now, according to which version of the story you find most to your liking, he either pointed to the stain and said, 'I say, chaps, what do you suppose this is?' Or he leapt to his feet screaming, 'It's blood! It's blood! Something horrible has happened here.' I tend to prefer the latter version, but perhaps it's only the alliteration that appeals to me.

The young men, feeling that someone inside the cottage might require assistance, pounded on the door. When they got no response, they tried the handle and found it locked. The windows all around the building were also locked. They broke the glass in a window, unlocked it, and they all climbed through.

In the hallway leading to the front door they found Andrea Maples, in what was described as 'a state of undress,' lying in a pool of blood — presumably her own, as she had been badly beaten about the head. Blood splatters covered the walls and ceiling. A short distance away from the body lay what was presumably the murder weapon: a mahogany cane with a brass duck's head handle.

One of the men immediately cycled off to the police station and returned with a police sergeant and two constables. When they ascertained that the hard wood cane belonged to Professor Maples, and that he carried it about with him constantly, the policemen crossed the lawn to the main house and interviewed the professor, who was having breakfast. At the conclusion of the interview, the sergeant placed Maples under arrest and sent one of the constables off to acquire a carriage in which the professor could be conveyed to the police station.

It was about four in the afternoon when Sherlock Holmes came banging at my study door. 'You've heard, of course,' he said, flinging himself into my armchair. 'What are we to do?'

'I've heard,' I said. 'And what have we to do with it?'

'That police sergeant, Meeks is his name, has arrested Professor Maples for the murder of his wife.'

'So I've heard.'

'He conducted no investigation, did not so much as glance at the surroundings, and failed to leave a constable behind to secure the area, so that, as soon as the rain lets up, hordes of the morbidly curious will trample about the cottage and the lawn and destroy whatever evidence there is to be found.'

'Did he?' I asked. 'And how do you know so much about it?'

'I was there,' Holmes said. At my surprised look, he shook his head. 'Oh, no, not at the time of the murder, whenever that was. When the constable came around for the carriage to take Professor Maples away, I happened to be in the stables. The hostler, Biggs is his name, is an expert single-stick fighter, and I've been taking lessons from him on occasional mornings when he has the time. So when they returned to the professor's house, Biggs drove and I sat in the carriage with the constable, who told me all about it.'

'I imagine he'll be talking about it for some time,' I commented. 'Murders are not exactly common around here.'

'Just so. Well, I went along thinking I might be of some use to Lucy. After all, her sister had just been murdered.'

'Thoughtful of you,' I said.

'Yes. Well, she wouldn't see me. Wouldn't see anyone. Just stayed in her room. Can't blame her, I suppose. So I listened to the sergeant questioning Professor Maples — and a damned poor job he did of it, if I'm any judge — and then went out and looked over the area — the two houses and the space between — to see if I could determine what happened. I also examined Andrea Maples's body as best I could from the doorway. I was afraid that if I got any closer Sergeant Meeks would notice and chase me away.'

'And did you determine what happened?'

'I may have,' Holmes said. 'If you'd do me the favor of taking a walk with me, I'd like to show you what I've found. I believe I have a good idea of what took place last night — or at least some of the salient details. I've worked it out from the traces on the ground and a few details in the cottage that the sergeant didn't bother with. It seems to me that much more can be done in the investigation of crimes than the police are accustomed to do. But I'd like your opinion. Tell me what you think.'

I pulled my topcoat on. 'Show me,' I said.

The drizzle was steady and cold, the ground was soggy, and by the time we arrived at the house the body had been removed; all of which reduced the number of curious visitors to two reporters who, having stomped about the cottage but failing to gain admittance to the main house, were huddled in a gig pulled up to the front door, waiting for someone to emerge who could be coaxed into a statement.

The main house and the cottage both fronted Barleymore Road, but as the road curved around a stand of trees between the two, the path through the property was considerably shorter. It was perhaps thirty yards from the house to the cottage by the path, and perhaps a little more than twice that by the road. I did measure the distance at the time, but I do not recollect the precise numbers.

We went around to the back of the house and knocked at the pantry door. After a few seconds' scrutiny through a side window, we were admitted by the maid.

'It's you, Mr. Holmes,' she said, stepping aside to let us in. 'Ain't it horrible? I've been waiting by the back door here for the man with the bunting, who's supposed to arrive shortly.'

'Bunting?'

'That's right. The black bunting which we is to hang in the windows, as is only proper, considering. Ain't it horrible? We should leave the doors and windows open, in respect of the dead, only the mistress's body has been taken away, and the master has been taken away, and it's raining, and those newspaper people will come in and pester Miss Lucy if the door is open. And then there's the murderer just a-waiting out there somewhere, and who knows what's on his mind.'

'So you don't think Professor Maples killed his wife?' I asked.

The maid looked at me, and then at Holmes, and then back at me. 'This is Mr. Moriarty, Willa,' Holmes told her. 'He's my friend, and a lecturer in Mathematics at the college.'

'Ah,' she said. 'It's a pleasure, sir.' And she bobbed a rudimentary curtsey in my direction. 'No, sir, I don't think the professor killed the Missus. Why would he do that?'

'Why, indeed,' I said.

'Miss Lucy is in the drawing room,' Willa told Holmes. 'I'll tell her you're here.'

'I see you're well known here,' I said to Holmes as the maid left.

41

'I have had the privilege of escorting Miss Lucy to this or that over the past few months,' Holmes replied a little stiffly, as though I were accusing him of something dishonorable. 'Our relationship has been very proper at all times.'

I repressed a desire to say 'how unfortunate,' as I thought he would take it badly.

Lucinda came out to the hall to meet us. She seemed quite subdued, but her eyes were bright and her complexion was feverish. 'How good — how nice to see you, Sherlock,' she said quietly, offering him her hand. 'And you're Mr. Moriarty, Sherlock's friend.'

Holmes and I both mumbled something comforting.

'I'm sorry I didn't see you when you arrived earlier, Sherlock,' Lucy told him, leading us into the sitting room and waving us to a pair of well-stuffed chairs. 'I was not in a fit condition to see anyone.'

'I quite understand,' Holmes said.

'I am pleased that you have come to the defense of my — of Professor Maples,'

Lucy said, lowering herself into a straight-back chair opposite Holmes. 'How anyone could suspect him of murdering my dear sister Andrea is quite beyond my comprehension.'

'I have reason to believe that he is, indeed, innocent, Lucy dear,' Holmes told her. 'I am about to take my friend Mr. Moriarty over the grounds to show him what I have found, and to see whether he agrees with my conclusions.'

'And your conclusions,' Lucy asked, 'what are they? Who do you believe committed this dreadful crime?'

'You have no idea?' I asked.

Lucinda recoiled as though I had struck her. 'How could I?' she asked.

'I didn't mean to startle you,' I said. 'Did your sister have any enemies?'

'Certainly not,' Lucy said. 'She was outgoing, and warm, and friendly, and loved by all.'

'Andrea went to the cottage to meet someone,' Holmes said. 'Do you have any idea who it was?'

'None,' Lucy said. 'I find this whole thing quite shocking.' She lowered her head into her hands. 'Quite shocking.'

After a moment Lucy raised her head. 'I have prepared a small traveling-bag of Professor Maples' things. A change of linen, a shirt, a couple of collars, some handkerchiefs, his shaving-cup and razor.'

'I don't imagine they'll let him have his razor,' Holmes commented.

'Oh!' Lucy said. 'I hadn't thought of that.'

'I may be wrong,' Holmes said. 'I will enquire.'

'Could I ask you to bring the bag to him?' Lucy rose. 'I have it right upstairs.'

We followed her upstairs to the master bedroom to collect the bag. The room was an image of masculine disorder, with Professor Maples' bed — they for some reason had separate beds, with a night-table between — rumpled and the bed clothes strewn about. Clothing was hung over various articles of furniture, and bureau drawers were pulled open. Maples had dressed hastily, presumably under police supervision, before being hauled off to the police station. Andrea's bed was neat and tight, and it was evident that she had not slept in it the night before.

I decided to take a quick look in the other five rooms leading off the hall. I thought I would give Holmes and Miss Lucy their moment of privacy if they desired to use it.

One of the rooms, fairly large and with a canopied bed, was obviously Lucy's. It was feminine without being overly frilly, and extremely, almost fussily, neat. There were two wardrobes in the room, across from each other, each with a collection of shoes on the bottom and a variety of female garments above.

I closed Lucy's door and knocked on the door across the hall. Getting no answer, I pushed the door open. It was one of the two rooms rented by the boarder, Crisboy, furnished as a sitting-room, and I could see the door to the bedroom to the left. The young athletic instructor was sitting at his writing desk, his shoulders stooped, and his face buried in his arms on the desk. 'Crisboy?' I said. 'Sorry, I didn't know you were here.' Which seemed a poor excuse for bursting in on a man, but my curiosity was probably inexcusable if it came to that.

He sat up and turned around. 'No matter,' he said, using a small towel he was holding to wipe his face, which was red and puffy from crying. 'Is there any news?' he asked me.

'Not that I am aware of,' I said.

'A heck of a thing,' he said. 'That police person thinks that John — Professor Maples — killed Andrea. How could he think that? Professor Maples couldn't hurt anyone. Insult them, yes; criticize them, yes; pierce them with barbs of — of — irony, yes. But hit anyone with a stick? Never!'

I backed out of Crisboy's sitting room with some murmured comment and closed the door. The hall door to the left was now identified as Crisboy's bedroom. The door to the right turned out to be Andrea's dressing room, with a small couch, a bureau, a dressing-table, and a connecting door to the master bedroom. The remaining door led to the lavatory.

Holmes emerged from the master bedroom with the traveling-bag thrust under his arm, shook hands with Lucy, and we went downstairs and out the back door.

'Here, this way,' Holmes said, taking me around to the side of the house. 'There are markings on the path that, I believe, give some insight into what happened here. I have covered them over with some planks I found by the side of the house, to prevent them being washed away or tramped over.'

'Clever,' I said.

'Elementary,' he replied.

Holmes had placed four pieces of planking on the path between the house and the cottage. We paused at the one nearest the house. 'The police theory — the theory of Sergeant Meeks — is that Andrea Maples left the house to have an assignation at the cottage with an unknown suitor — if a man who trysts with a married woman may be called a suitor. They are trying to determine whom he is. Professor Maples, awakening sometime during the night and finding his wife absent, went to the cottage, caught her as the suitor was leaving, or just after he left, realized what had happened by the state of her clothes, if not by other, ah, indications, and, in an uncontrollable rage, beat her to death with his walking-stick.'

I nodded. 'That's about the way it was told to me.'

'That story is contravened by the evidence,' Holmes declared carefully lifting the plank. 'Observe the footsteps.'

The plank covered a partial line of footsteps headed from the house to the cottage, and at least one footstep headed back to the house. The imprint in all cases was that of a woman's shoe.

'Note this indentation,' Holmes said, pointing out a round hole about three-quarters of an inch across and perhaps an inch deep that was slightly forward and to the right of an out-bound shoe imprint.

He sprinted over to the next plank and moved it, and then the next. 'Look here,' he called. 'And here, and here. The same pattern.'

'Yes,' I said, 'I see.' I bent down and examined several of the footsteps closely, marking off the measurement from toe to heel and across the width of the imprint in my pocket notebook, and doing a rough sketch of what I saw, shielding the notebook as best I could from the slight drizzle.

'Notice that none of the footsteps in either direction were left by a man,' Holmes said.

'Yes,' I said, 'I can see that.' There were three sets of footsteps, two leading from the house to the cottage, and one returning.

'It proves that Professor Maples did not kill his wife,' Holmes asserted.

'It certainly weakens the case against him,' I admitted.

'Come now,' Holmes said. 'Surely you see that the entire case is predicated on the syllogism that, as Maples is never without his walking stick, and as his walking stick was used to kill Andrea Maples, then Maples must have murdered his wife.'

'So it would seem,' I agreed.

'A curious stick,' Holmes told me. 'I had occasion to examine it once. Did you know that it is actually a sword-cane?'

'I did not know that,' I said.

'I believe that it will prove an important fact in the case,' Holmes told me.

'I assume that your conclusion is that Professor Maples was without his walking stick last night.'

'That's right. Andrea Maples took it to the cottage herself. The indentations by her footsteps show that.'

'What is it that you think happened?' I asked Holmes.

'As you've noted, there are three sets of footsteps,' Holmes said. 'Two going from the house to the cottage, and one returning to the house. As you can see, they are the footprints of a woman, and, carefully as I looked, I could find no indication of any footprints made by a man. One of the sets going seems to be slightly different in the indentation of the heel than the other sets. The returning set seems to be made up of footsteps that are further apart, and leave a deeper imprint than the others. I would say from examining them that Andrea Maples went to the cottage to meet someone. Before he arrived, she decided to arm herself and so she rushed back to the house and changed shoes — perhaps the first pair had been soaked by her stepping in a puddle — and then took her husband's walking stick — which she knew to be actually a sword-cane — and returned to the cottage.'

'And the person she was planning to meet?'

'He must have come by the road, as there are no markings on the path. But Professor Maples would surely have come by the path.'

'So she thought herself to be in some danger?'

'So I would read it.'

'So you would have it that it was not a romantic tryst?'

'Perhaps it had been,' Holmes suggested. 'Perhaps she had decided to break off an affair with some person, and she knew him to have a violent nature. In the event it seems that she was correct.'

We had reached the cottage and, finding the back door unlocked, entered the small back pantry leading to the kitchen. Holmes dropped the traveling-bag by the door and lay his topcoat and hat over a kitchen chair, and I followed suit.

'That would explain why she failed to wake up her husband and returned to the cottage by herself, although she believed herself in some danger,' I said. 'It neatly ties up most of the known facts. But I'm afraid that you won't be able to convince the police that you're right.'

'Why not?'

'There's the fact of the disarray of Andrea Maples's clothing. As I understand it she was in her undergarments, and seems to have been dressing. It indicates that the meeting with her mysterious friend was, ah, friendly.'

'Perhaps he forced himself on her.'

'Perhaps. But then one would expect her clothing to be not merely loosened or removed, but stretched or torn. I did not hear that this was so. Did you have an opportunity to examine the woman's clothing?'

'Yes, I paid particular attention to the state of her clothing. She was wearing a petticoat and an over-something — another frilly white garment covering the upper part of her body. I am not very expert in the names of women's garments.'

'Nor am I,' I said. 'I assume the remainder of her clothing was somewhere about?'

'It was in the bedroom.'

We entered the parlor. The shades were drawn, keeping out even the weak light from the overcast sky. Holmes struck a match and lit an oil-lamp, which was sitting on a nearby table. The flickering light cast grotesque shadows about the room, creating a nebulous sense of oppression and doom. Or perhaps it was just the knowledge of what had recently transpired here that gave the room its evil character. 'There,' Holmes said, pointing to a large irregularly-shaped bloodstain on the floor by the front door. 'There is where she lay. She came from the bedroom, as the rest of her clothing was there, and was attacked in the parlor.'

'Curious,' I said.

'Really?' Holmes replied. 'How so?'

The question was not destined to be answered, at least not then. At that moment the front door banged open and a police sergeant of immense girth, a round, red face, and a majestic handlebar mustache stomped down the hall and into the room. 'Here now,' he boomed. 'What are you gentlemen doing in here, if I might ask?'

'Sergeant Meeks,' Holmes said. 'You've returned to the scene of the crime. Perhaps you are going to take my suggestion after all.'

Meeks looked at Holmes with an air of benevolent curiosity. 'And what suggestion might that be, young man?'

'I mentioned to you that it might be a good idea to post a constable here to keep the curiosity-seekers from wandering about. It was when you were escorting Professor Maples into the carriage to take him away.'

'Why so it was, Mr., ah, — '

'Holmes. And this is Mr. Moriarty.'

Meeks gave me a perfunctory nod, and turned his attention back to Holmes. 'Yes, Mr. Holmes. So it was, and so you did. We of the regular constabulary are always grateful for any hints or suggestions as we might get from young gentlemen such as yourself. You also said something about preserving the foot-marks along the lane out back, as I remember.'

'That's right.'

'Well I went to look at them foot-marks of yours, Mr. Holmes, lifting up a couple of them boards you put down and peering under. They was just what you said they was — foot-marks; and I thanks you kindly.'

'From your attitude I can see that you don't attach much importance to the imprints,' Holmes commented, not allowing himself to be annoyed by the sergeant's words or his sneering tone.

'We always try to plot a straight and true course when we're investigating a case,' the sergeant explained. 'There are always facts and circumstances around that don't seem to fit in. And that's because, if you'll excuse my saying so, they have nothing to do with the case.'

'But perhaps there are times when some of these facts that you ignore actually present a clearer explanation of what really happened,' Holmes suggested.

'For example, Sergeant, I'm sure you noticed that the footsteps were all made by a woman. Not a single imprint of a man's foot on that path.'

'If you say so, Mr. Holmes. I can't say that I examined them all that closely.'

Holmes nodded. 'If what I say is true,' he said, 'doesn't that suggest anything to you?'

Sergeant Meeks sighed a patient sigh. 'It would indicate that the accused did not walk on the path. Perhaps he went by the road. Perhaps he flew. It don't really matter how he got to the cottage, it only matters what he did after he arrived.'

'Did you notice the imprint of the walking stick next to the woman's footsteps?' Holmes asked. 'Does that tell you nothing?'

'Nothing,' the sergeant agreed. 'She may have had another walking stick, or perhaps the branch from a tree.'

Holmes shrugged. 'I give up,' he said.

'You'd be better off leaving the detecting to the professionals, young man,' Meeks said. 'We've done some investigating on our own already, don't think we haven't. And what we've heard pretty well wraps up the case against Professor Maples. I'm sorry, but there you have it.'

'What have you heard?' Holmes demanded.

'Never you mind. That will all come out at the inquest, and that's soon enough. Now you'd best be getting out of here, the pair of you. I am taking your advice to the extent of locking the cottage up and having that broken window boarded over. We don't want curiosity seekers walking away with the furniture.'

We retrieved our hats and coats and the bag with Professor Maples' fresh clothing and left the cottage. The rain had stopped, but dusk was approaching and a cold wind gusted through the trees. Holmes and I walked silently back to the college, each immersed in our own thoughts: Holmes presumably wondering what new facts had come to light, and trying to decide how to get his information before the authorities; I musing on the morality of revealing to Holmes, or to others, what I had discerned, and from that what I had surmised, or letting matters proceed without my intervention.

Holmes left me at the college to continue on to the police station, and I returned to my rooms.

The inquest was held two days later in the chapel of, let me call it, St. Elmo's College, one of our sister colleges making up the university. The chapel, a large gothic structure with pews that would seat several hundred worshipers, had been borrowed for this more secular purpose in expectation of a rather large turnout of spectators; in which expectation the coroner was not disappointed.

The coroner, a local squire named Sir George Quick, was called upon to perform this function two or three times a year. But usually it was for an unfortunate who had drowned in the canal or fallen off a roof. Murders were quite rare in the area; or perhaps most murderers were more subtle than whoever had done in Andrea Maples.

Holmes and I sat in the audience and watched the examination proceed. Holmes had gone to the coroner before the jury was seated and asked if he

58

could give evidence. When he explained what he wanted to say, Sir George sent him back to his seat. What he had to offer was not evidence, Sir George explained to him, but his interpretation of the evidence. 'It is for the jury to interpret the evidence offered,' Sir George told him, 'not for you or I.' Holmes's face was red with anger and mortification, and he glowered at the courtroom and everyone in it. I did my best not to notice.

Lucinda was in the front row, dressed in black. Her face wooden, she stared straight ahead through the half-veil that covered her eyes, and did not seem to be following anything that was happening around her. Crisboy sat next to her, wearing a black armband and a downcast expression. Professor Maples was sitting to one side, with a bulky constable sitting next to him and another sitting behind him. He had a bemused expression on his face, as though he couldn't really take any of this seriously.

Sir George informed the assemblage that he was going to proceed in an orderly manner, and that he would tolerate no fiddle-faddle and then called his first witness. It turned out to be the young bicyclist with the sticky fingers. 'I could see that it was blood,' he said, 'and that it had come from beneath the door — from inside the house.'

Then he described how he and his companions broke a window to gain entrance, and found Andrea Maples' body sprawled on the floor by the front door.

'And how was she dressed?' the coroner asked.

'She was not dressed, sir,' came the answer.

A murmur arose in the audience, and the young man blushed and corrected himself. 'That is to say, she was not *completely* dressed. She had on her, ah, undergarments, but not her dress.'

'Shoes?' the coroner asked, with the bland air of one who is called upon to discuss semi-naked ladies every day.

'I don't believe so, sir.'

'That will be all,' the coroner told him, 'unless the jury have any questions?' he added, looking over at the six townsmen in the improvised jury box.

The foreman of the jury, an elderly man with a well-developed set of mutton-chop whiskers, nodded and gazed out at the witness. 'Could you tell us,' he asked slowly, 'what color were these undergarments?'

'White,' the young man said.

'Now then,' Sir George said, staring severely at the foreman, 'that will be enough of that!'

Sergeant Meeks was called next. He sat in the improvised witness box hat in hand, his uniform and his face having both been buffed to a high shine, the very model of English propriety. The coroner led him through having been called, and arriving at the scene with his two constables, and examining the body.

'And then what did you do, sergeant?'

'After sending Constable Gough off to Beachamshire to notify the police surgeon, I thoroughly examined the premises to see whether I could ascertain what had occurred on the, ah, premises.'

'And what were your conclusions?'

'The deceased was identified to me as Mrs. Andrea Maples, wife of Professor Maples, who lived in the main house on the same property. She was dressed — '

'Yes, yes, sergeant,' Sir George interrupted. 'We've heard how she was dressed. Please go on.'

'Very good, sir. She had been dead for some time when I examined her. I would put her death at between seven and ten hours previous, based on my experience. Which placed the time of her death at sometime around midnight.'

'And on what do you base that conclusion?'

'The blood around the body was pretty well congealed, but not completely in the deeper pools, and the body appeared to be fairly well along into *rigor mortis* at that time.

'Very observant, sergeant. And what else did you notice?'

'The murder weapon was lying near the body. It was a hardwood walking stick with a duck's-head handle. It had some of the victim's blood on it, and a clump of the victim's hair was affixed to the duck's head in the beak area. The stick was identified by one of the bicyclists who was still present as being the property of Professor Maples, husband of the victim.'

'And what did you do then?'

'I proceeded over to the main house to question Professor Maples, who was just sitting down to breakfast when I arrived. I told him of his wife's death, and he affected to be quite disturbed at the news. I then asked him to produce his walking stick, and he spend some time affecting to look for it. I then placed him under arrest and sent Constable Parfry for a carriage to take the professor to the station house.'

'Here, now!' a short, squat juror with a walrus moustache that covered his face from below his nose to below his chin, shifted in his seat and leaned belligerently forward. 'What made you arrest the professor at that there moment? It seems to me that whoever the Maples woman was having an assigerna . . . was meeting at this here cottage in the middle of the night was more likely to have done her in.'

'Now, now, we'll get to that,' the

coroner said, fixing the fractious juror with a stern eye. 'I'm trying to lay out the facts of the case in an orderly manner. We'll get to that soon enough.'

The next witness was the police surgeon, who testified that the decedent had met her death as a result of multiple blunt-force blows to the head and shoulders. He couldn't say just which blow killed her, any one of several could have. And, yes, the duck-headed cane presented in evidence could have been the murder weapon.

Sir George nodded. So much for those who wanted information out of its proper order. Now . . .

Professor Maples was called next. The audience looked expectant. He testified that he had last seen his wife at about nine o'clock on the night she was killed. After which he had gone to bed, and, as he had been asleep, had not been aware of her absence.

'You did not note that she was missing when you awoke, or when you went down to breakfast?' Sir George asked.

'I assumed she had gone out early,'

Maples replied. 'She went out early on occasion. I certainly didn't consider foul play. One doesn't, you know.'

Professor Maples was excused, and the audience looked disappointed.

An acne-laden young man named Cramper was called up next. He was, he explained, employed at the local public house, the Red Garter, as a sort of general assistant. On the night of the murder he had been working unusually late, shifting barrels of ale from one side of the cellar to the other. 'It were on account of the rats,' he explained.

Sir George, wisely, did not pursue that answer any further. 'What time was it when you started for home?' he asked.

'Must have been going on for midnight, one side or 'nother.'

Sir George stared expectantly at Cramper, and Cramper stared back complacently at Sir George.

'Well?' the coroner said finally.

'Well? Oh, what happened whilst I walked home. Well, I saw someone emerging from the old Wilstone cottage.'

'That's the cottage where the murder

65

took place?' Sir George prompted.

'Aye, that's the one aright. Used to be a gent named Wilstone lived there. Still comes back from time to time, I believe.'

'Ah!' said Sir George. 'And this person you saw coming from the, ah, old Wilstone cottage?'

'Happens I know the gent. Name of Faulting. He teaches jumping and squatting, or some such, over by the college field building.'

There was a murmur from the audience, which Sir George quashed with a look.

'And you could see clearly who the gentleman was, even though it was the middle of the night?'

'Ever so clearly. Aye, sir.'

'And how was that?'

'Well, there were lights on in the house, and his face were all lit up by them lights.'

'Well,' Sir George said, looking first at the jury and then at the audience. 'We will be calling Mr. Faulting next, to verify Mr. Cramper's story. And he will, gentlemen and, er, ladies. He will. Now, what else did you see, Mr. Cramper?'

'You mean in the house?'

'That's right. In the house.'

'Well, I saw the lady in question — the lady who got herself killed.'

'You saw Mrs. Maples in the house?'

'Aye, that's so. She were at the door, saying goodbye to this Faulting gent.'

'So she was alive and well at that time?'

'Aye. That she were.'

The jury foreman leaned forward. 'And how were she dressed?' he called out, and then stared defiantly at the coroner, who had turned to glare at him.

'It were only for a few seconds that I saw her before she closed the door,' Cramper replied. 'She were wearing something white, I didn't much notice what.'

'Yes, thank you,' you're excused,' Sir George said.

Mr. Faulting was called next, and he crept up to the witness chair like a man who knew he was having a bad dream, but didn't know how to get out of it. He admitted having been Andrea Maples' night visitor. He was not very happy about it, and most of his answers were mumbles, despite Sir George's constant admonitions to speak up. Andrea had, he informed the coroner's court, invited him to meet her in the cottage at ten o'clock.

'What about her husband?' the coroner demanded.

'I asked her that,' Faulting said. 'She laughed. She told me that he wouldn't object; that I was free to ask him if I liked. I, uh, I didn't speak with him.'

'No,' the coroner said, 'I don't imagine you did.'

Faulting was the last witness. The coroner reminded the jury that they were not to accuse any person of a crime, even if they thought there had been a crime; that was a job for the criminal courts. They were merely to determine cause of death. After a brief consultation, the jury returned a verdict of unlawful death.

'Thank you,' Sir George said. 'You have done your duty. I assume,' he said, looking over at Sergeant Meeks, 'that there is no need for me to suggest a course of action to the police.'

'No, sir,' Meeks told him. 'Professor

Maples will be bound over for trial at the assizes.'

Sir George nodded. 'Quite right,' he said.

'Bah!' Holmes said to me in an undertone.

'You disagree?' I asked.

'I can think of a dozen ways Faulting could have pulled that trick,' he said. 'That young man — Cramper — didn't see Andrea Maples in the doorway, he saw a flash of something white.'

'Perhaps,' I said.

'Bah!' Holmes repeated.

When we left the building Miss Lucy came over to Holmes and pulled him away, talking to him in an earnest undertone. I walked slowly back to my rooms, trying to decide what to do. I disliked interfering with the authorities in their attempted search for justice, and I probably couldn't prove what I knew to be true, but could I stand by and allow an innocent man to be convicted of murder? And Maples would surely be convicted if he came to trial. There was no real evidence against him, but he had the appearance of guilt, and that's enough to convince nine juries out of ten.

About two hours later Holmes came over, his eyes shining. 'Miss Lucy is a fine woman,' he told me.

'Really?' I said.

'We talked for a while about her sister. That is, she tried to talk about Andrea, but she kept breaking down and crying before she could finish a thought.'

'Not surprising,' I said.

'She asked me if I thought Professor Maples was guilty,' Holmes told me. 'I said I was convinced he was not. She asked me if I thought he would be convicted if he came to trial. I thought I'd better be honest. I told her it seemed likely.'

'You told her true,' I commented.

'She is convinced of his innocence, even though it is her own sister who was killed. Many — most — people would allow emotion to override logic. And she wants to help him. She said, 'Then I know what I must do,' and she went off to see about hiring a lawyer.'

'She said that?' I asked.

'She did.'

'Holmes, think carefully. Did she say she was going to hire a lawyer?'

Holmes was momentarily startled at my question. 'Well, let's see. She said she knew what she must do, and I said he's going to need the best lawyer and the best barrister around to clear himself of this, for all that we know he is not guilty.'

'And?'

'And then she said she would not allow him to be convicted. And she — well — she kissed me on the cheek, and she said, 'Goodbye, Mr. Holmes, you have been a good friend.' And she hurried off.'

'How long ago did she leave you?'

'Possibly an hour, perhaps a bit longer.'

I jumped to my feet. 'Come, Holmes,' I said, 'we must stop her.'

'Stop her?'

'Before she does something foolish. Come, there's no time to waste!'

'Does what?' he asked, hurrying after me as I hastened down the hall, pulling my coat on.

'Just come!' I said. 'Perhaps I'm wrong.'

We raced out of the college and over to Barleymore Road, and continued in the direction of the Maples' house at a fast walk. It took about ten minutes to get there, and I pushed through the front door without bothering to knock.

Mr. Crisboy was sitting in the parlor, staring at the wall opposite, a study in suspended motion. In one hand was a spoon, in the other a small bottle. When we entered the room he slowly put both objects down. 'Professor Maples depends on this fluid,' he said. 'Two spoons full before each meal.' He held the bottle up for our inspection. The label read: *Peals Patented Magical Elixir of Health.* 'Do you think they'd let me bring him a few bottles?'

'I'm sure they would,' I told him. 'Do you know where Lucy is?'

'She's upstairs in her room,' Crisboy told me. 'She is quite upset. But of course, we're all quite upset. She asked not to be disturbed.'

I made for the staircase, Holmes close behind me. 'Why this rush?' He demanded. 'We can't just barge in on her.'

'We must,' I said. I pounded at her door, but there was no answer. The door was locked. I put my shoulder against it. After the third push it gave, and I stumbled into the room, Holmes close behind me.

There was an overturned chair in the middle of the room. From a hook in the ceiling that had once held a chandelier, dangled the body of Lucy Moys.

'My God!' Holmes exclaimed.

Holmes righted the chair and pulled a small clasp knife from his pocket. I held the body steady while Holmes leaped up on the chair and sawed at the rope until it parted. We lay her carefully on the bed. It was clear from her white face and bulging, sightless eyes that she was beyond reviving. Holmes nonetheless cut the loop from around her neck. 'Horrible,' he said. 'And you knew this was going to happen? But why? There's no reason — '

'Every reason,' I said. 'No, I didn't predict this, certainly not this quickly, but I did think she might do something foolish.'

'But — '

'She must have left a note,' I said.

We covered her body with a blanket, and Holmes went over to the writing desk. 'Yes,' he said. 'There's an envelope here addressed to 'The Police.' And a second one — it's addressed to me!'

He ripped it open. After a few seconds he handed it to me.

Sherlock,

*It could have been different
had I been different.
I like you tremendously.
Think well of me.
I'm so sorry.*

Lucy

'I don't understand,' Sherlock Holmes said. 'What does it mean? Why did she do this?'

'The letter to the police,' I said, 'what does it say?'

He opened it.

To whoever reads this —

I am responsible for the death of my sister Andrea. I killed her in a jealous rage. I cannot live with myself, and I cannot allow Professor Maples, a sweet and innocent man, to suffer for my crime. This is best for all concerned.

Lucinda Moys

'I don't understand,' Holmes said. 'She was jealous of Faulting? But I didn't think she even knew Faulting very well.'

'She kept her secrets,' I said, 'even onto death.'

'What secrets?'

'This household,' I said, gesturing around me, 'holds one big secret that is, you might say, made up of several smaller secrets.'

'You knew that she had done it — that she had killed her sister?'

'I thought so, yes.' I patted him on the shoulder, and he flinched as though my touch was painful. 'Let us go downstairs now,' I said.

'You go,' Holmes said. 'I'll join you in a few minutes.'

I left Holmes staring down at the blanket-covered body on the bed, and went down to the parlor. 'Lucy has committed suicide,' I told Crisboy, who had put the bottle down but was still staring at the wall opposite. 'She left a note. She killed Andrea.'

'Ahhh!' he said. 'Then they'll be letting the professor go.'

'Yes,' I said.

'She'd been acting strange the past few days. But with what happened, I never thought . . . Hung herself?'

'Yes,' I said. 'Someone must go to the police station.'

'Of course.' Crisboy got up. 'I'll go.' He went into the hall and took his overcoat off the peg. 'Ahhh. Poor thing.' He went out the door.

About ten minutes later Holmes came down. 'How did you know?' he asked.

'The footsteps that you preserved so carefully,' I said. 'There were three lines: two going out to the cottage and one coming back. The single one going out was wearing different shoes, and it — she — went first. I could tell because some of

76

the prints from the other set overlapped the first. And it was the second set going out that had the indentations from the walking stick. So someone — some woman — went out after Andrea Maples, and that woman came back. She went out with the walking stick and came back without it.'

'I missed that,' Holmes said.

'It's easier to tell than to observe,' I told him.

'I had made up my mind about what I was going to find before I went to look,' he said. 'The deductive process suffers from preconceptions.'

'It's a matter of eliminating the impossible,' I told him. 'Then whatever remains, however improbable, must be the truth.'

'I shall remember that,' he said. 'I still cannot fathom that Lucy was that jealous of Andrea.'

'She was, but not in the way you imagine,' I told him.

'What do you mean?'

'Do you remember that I suggested that you notice Lucinda's ears?'

'Yes.' Holmes looked puzzled. 'They looked like — ears.'

'Their shape was quite distinctive, and quite different from those of Andrea. The basic shape of the ear seems to be constant within a family. This was a reasonable indication that Andrea and Lucinda were not really sisters.'

'Not really sisters? Then they were — what?'

'They were lovers,' I told him. 'There are women who fall in love with other women, just as there are men who fall in love with other men. The ancient Greeks thought it quite normal.'

'Lovers?'

'Andrea preferred women to men, and Lucinda was her, ah, mate.'

'But — Professor Maples is her husband.'

'I assume it was truly a marriage of convenience. If you look at the bedrooms it is clear that Andrea and Lucy usually shared a bedroom — Lucy's — as they both have quantities of clothing in it. And I would assume that Professor Maples and Mr. Crisboy have a similar arrangement.'

'You think the professor and Crisboy — but they . . . '

'A German professor named Ulrichs has coined a word for such unions; he calls them homo-sexual. In some societies they are accepted, and in some they are condemned. We live in the latter.'

Holmes sat down in the straight-back chair. 'That is so,' he said. 'So you think they derived this method of keeping their relationships concealed?'

'I imagine the marriage, if there was a marriage, and Andrea's adopting Lucy as her 'sister' was established well before the ménage moved here. It was the ideal solution, each protecting the other from the scorn of society and the sting of the laws against sodomy and such behavior.'

'But Andrea went to the cottage to have, ah, intimate relations with Faulting.'

'She liked to flirt, you must have observed that. And she obviously wasn't picky as to which gender she flirted with, or with which gender she, let us say, consummated her flirting. There are women like that, many of them it seems, unusually attractive and, ah, compelling. Augustus Caesar's daughter Julia seems to have been one of them, according to Suetonius. Andrea found Faulting attractive, and was determined to have him. My guess is that she and Lucy had words about it, but Andrea went to meet Faulting anyway, while Lucy remained in her room and worked herself into a jealous rage. She didn't intend to kill Andrea; that's shown by the fact that she didn't open the sword-cane, although she must have known about it.'

Holmes was silent for a minute, and I could see some powerful emotion growing within him. 'You had this all figured out,' he said, turning to me, his words tight and controlled.

'Much of it,' I admitted. 'But don't berate yourself for missing it. I was familiar with the idea of homo-sexuality through my reading, and several acquaintances of mine have told me of such relationships. I had the knowledge and you didn't.'

But I had misjudged the direction of Holmes' thoughts. The fury in him suddenly exploded. 'You could have stopped this,' he screamed. 'You let it happen!'

I backed away to avoid either of us doing something we would later regret. 'I knew nothing of Andrea's tryst,' I told him, 'nor Lucinda's fury.'

Holmes took a deep breath. 'No,' he said, 'you couldn't have stopped the murder, but you could have stopped Lucy's suicide. Clearly you knew what she intended.'

'You credit me with a prescience I do not possess,' I told him.

'You were fairly clear on what she intended an hour after the event,' he said. 'Why couldn't you have rushed out here before?'

'I don't know,' I told him. 'Until you told me what she had said to you, it didn't strike me — '

'It didn't strike you!'

'You spoke to her yourself,' I said, 'and yet you guessed nothing.'

'I didn't know what you knew,' he said. 'I was a fool. But you — what were you?'

I had no answer for him. Perhaps I

should have guessed what Lucy intended. Perhaps I did guess. Perhaps, on some unconscious level I weighed the options of her ending her own life, or of her facing an English jury, and then being taken out one cold morning, and having the hood tied around her head and the heavy hemp rope around her neck, and hearing a pusillanimous parson murmuring homilies at her until they sprang the trap.

* * *

A few minutes later the police arrived. The next day Professor Maples was released from custody and returned home. Within a month he and Crisboy had packed up and left the college. Although nothing was ever officially said about their relationship, the rumors followed them to Maples' next position, and to the one after that, until finally they left Britain entirely. I lost track of them after that. Holmes left the college at the end of the term. I believe that, after taking a year off, he subsequently enrolled at Cambridge.

Holmes has never forgiven me for what he believes I did. He has also, it would seem, never forgiven the fair sex for the transgressions of Lucinda Moys. I did not at the time realize the depth of his feelings toward her. Perhaps he didn't either. His feeling toward me is unfortunate and has led, over the years, to some monstrous accusations on his part. I am no saint. Indeed, as it happens I eventually found myself on the other side of the law as often as not. I am pleased to call myself England's first consulting criminal, as I indulge in breaking the laws of my country to support my scientific endeavors. But when Holmes calls me 'the Napoleon of crime,' is he not perhaps seeing, through the mists of time, the blanket-covered body of that unfortunate girl whose death he blames on me? And could it be that he is reflecting on the fact that the first, perhaps the only, woman he ever loved was incapable of loving him in return?

At any rate, I issue one last stern warning to those of you who repeat

Holmes's foul canards about me in print, or otherwise: there are certain of the laws of our land that I embrace heartily, and the laws of libel and slander ride high on the list. Beware!

2

Reichenbach

You remember, I assume, the newspaper accounts of the accidental deaths of the consulting detective Sherlock Holmes and the eminent mathematician Professor James Moriarty at Kessel Falls at the River Reichenbach in Switzerland. Or perhaps you've read Dr. Watson's account of the confrontation at, as he called it, 'Reichenbach Falls' between Holmes and the 'master criminal' Moriarty. It seems that everyone in the English speaking world has read of, or at least heard of the incident. And then, you will recall, some three years later Holmes reappeared to Watson and explained his absence and supposed death in some detail. Well, I am here to tell you that almost every word of these accounts, including Holmes's recantation, is false, and I should know. I am Professor James Moriarty.

It is not the fault of the newspapers, who published with no more than their usual disregard for the facts, nor of Dr. Watson, who believed everything told to him by his friend and companion Sherlock Holmes. There can be no greater friend than one who believes whatever he is told no matter how strongly it is belied by the evidence to the contrary. Is that not, after all, the basis of most religion?

This, then, is an account of the events that led up to the disappearance, and what transpired for a short time afterward. I was going to say a 'true account,' but I refrained, because memory is faulty, and there were some facts that I was not privy to that might make a difference in the truth of what happened. It is, then, an account of the events as they appeared to me at the time.

It was on the evening of Wednesday, the 22nd of April, 1891, that Mr. Maws, my butler, ushered a man named Tippins into my study. A tall, thin, angular man wearing a black frock coat with red cuffs and pockets, and large brass buttons, he stood, top hat in hand, before my desk and peered at me through oversized gold spectacles. His nose, while not large enough to be truly grotesque, was the most prominent object on his face, possibly because of the web of red veins beneath the roseate skin. A brush mustache directly beneath the nose added character to the face, but it was not a character whose acquaintance I would have gone out of my way to make. 'I have come to you from Mr. Holmes,' he began. 'He requires your assistance, and has asked me to direct you to the secret location where he awaits you.'

I am not easily surprised. Indeed, I spend a good bit of time and effort making sure that I am not surprised. But I confess that, for a second, I was astounded. 'Holmes wants to see me? Is this some sort of trick?' I demanded.

He considered. 'Naw, I wouldn't think so,' he said finally. 'He's much too stout to indulge in that sort of tomfoolery, I should think.'

'Ah!' I said. 'Stout, is he? So it's Mr. *Mycroft* Holmes who desires my assistance.'

'Indeed,' Tippins agreed. 'Isn't that what I said?'

'I thought perhaps his brother . . . '

Tippins snorted. 'The consulting detective chap? What has he to do with foreign policy?'

'Foreign policy?' I inquired.

'Perhaps you'd best just go and find out for yourself,' Tippins suggested.

'To the Foreign Office?'

'Naw. Mr. Holmes don't want it known that he's meeting with you, so he has arranged for my services to get you to his, so-to-speak secret location.'

'Services?' I asked. 'What sort of services?'

He tapped himself on the chest. 'I'm a conniver,' he said.

'Interesting,' I allowed. 'You scheme and plot for Her Majesty's government?'

'I enable people to do necessary things in unusual ways, when the more usual ways are not available.' He smiled. 'I occasionally perform services for Mr. Holmes, but few others in Her Majesty's government have availed themselves of my services.'

'And what necessary service would you perform for me in your unorthodox fashion?' I asked him.

'Your house is being watched,' Tippins said.

I nodded. I had been aware of a steady watch being kept on my house for the past few weeks. 'No doubt by that very consulting detective chap you were mentioning,' I said.

'Mr. Holmes did not want it known that he was to speak with you,' Tippins explained, 'so he sent me.'

'I see,' I said. 'How are you going to get me there unseen?'

'I have a carriage waiting outside,' Tippins said, unbuttoning his frock coat. 'The driver knows where to go. You will leave here as me. I will await your return here, if you don't mind. I have brought a book.' He took off the frock coat and handed it to me. 'Put this on.'

'It is distinctive,' I said, examining the red pockets. 'But I'm not sure we look alike enough, ah, facially, for the masquerade to work.'

'Ah! There we have the crux of the

matter,' he told me. He reached for the gold frame of his glasses and carefully removed them from his face. With them came the red nose and the brush mustache. The face beneath was quite ordinary, and the nose was, if anything, rather small.

'Bless me!' I said, or perhaps it was a slightly stronger expression.

He smiled. 'Simple but effective,' he said. 'The watchers will see what they expect to see.'

I put on the glasses, with the accompanying nose and mustache, and shrugged into the coat.

'Here,' Tippins said, handing me his top hat. 'It will complete the illusion.'

And indeed it did. Wrapped in Tippins' frock coat and wearing much of what had been his face, I thrust the journal I had been reading into the coat pocket and left my house. I clambered into the waiting carriage, a sturdy but undistinguished hack, and the jarvey spoke to the horse, and we were on our way. I waited about ten minutes before removing the facial part of the disguise. Perhaps I shouldn't have taken it off so soon, but I felt foolish enough in the coat of several colors without wearing that nose one moment longer than I had to. I kept a careful eye out the rear window, but as far as I could tell no one was following us or taking an undue interest in our passage.

After several turns designed to force anyone following us to come into view, the jarvey took a fairly straight course to Regent's Park Road, turned off on a side street, and pulled to a stop in the middle of a block of flats. He hopped down from his perch and opened the carriage door for me. 'That door there,' he said, indicating a brown door much like all the other brown doors along the street. 'You're expected.'

It crossed my mind that this might be a trap. There are people in London who would rather see me dead than steal a million pounds, and one of them might have been inside that door instead of the rotund Mr. Holmes. But I have an instinct for such things, and this was both too elaborate and too commonplace to be anything other than what it seemed. So I pulled up the collar of my borrowed coat against the chill wind, crossed the walk, and pulled the bell-pull at the indicated doorway.

No more than three seconds later the door opened and a short woman of immense girth dressed as a maid gestured me in. Whether she was actually a maid, or some employee of the Foreign Service in masquerade I cannot say. 'This way, Professor Moriarty sir,' she said. 'You're expected.'

She showed me into a room that might have been the waiting room in some doctor's surgery, or for that matter the outer office of the booking agent for a music hall. There was a wide, well-worn black leather couch, several large and sturdy chairs, a heavy table of some dark wood, ill-lit by three wall sconces with the gas turned low and a window with heavy light-green muslin curtains, which were drawn. A deep throbbing sound came faintly into the room; I could discern neither the location nor the function of its agent. Some sort of machinery? On the right-hand wall, leading to the back of the house, a pair of double doors were drawn closed. 'Please wait,' she said. '*He* will be with you shortly.' The timbre of her voice changed when she said '*He*,' the added resonance giving the word importance, as though I were awaiting Aristotle or Charles Darwin himself. 'Please don't open the shades,' she added as she left the room.

I turned the gas light up in one of the wall sconces and settled into a chair beneath it, taking from my pocket the journal I had brought with me, *Das Astrophysische Journal der Universität Erlangen*, and immersing myself in its pages. The Austrians Joffe and Shostak have advanced the theory that the nebulosities observed through the larger telescopes are not some sort of interstellar gas, but actually vast clouds of stars much like our own Milky Way galaxy, seen at tremendous distances. If so — but I digress.

After a while I heard the door open and close, and I looked up to find Sherlock Holmes standing in the doorway. 'So!' he growled, looking down his thin, crooked nose at me. 'It was one of your tricks after all!' He thrust his walking stick in front of him like a child playing at dueling. 'I warn you that I am prepared for any eventuality.'

'How nice for you,' I said, folding my journal and putting it back into my pocket.

'Mr. Holmes,' said the broad maid from behind him. 'Please be seated. Your brother will be down directly.'

Holmes stalked over to a chair in the far side of the room and dropped lightly into it. 'We'll see,' he said, never taking his eyes off me. He flexed his walking stick, describing a series of shapes in the air before him, and then laid it across his knees.

The door opened again, and the large shape of Mycroft Holmes loomed into the room. 'Sherlock,' he said, 'Professor Moriarty. Good of you to come. Join me in the next room, where we can talk.'

'You invited *him*?' asked Sherlock, pointing a wavering walking stick in my direction. 'What were you thinking?'

'All in good time,' said Mycroft.

'Follow me.' He stomped through the waiting room and pulled open the double doors. The chamber thus revealed had once been the dining room of the house, but was now a conference room, with an oversized highly-polished mahogany table in the center, surrounded by heavy chairs of the same dark wood, upholstered in green leather. Around the periphery stood a row of filing cabinets, and a pair of small writing desks. A large chart cabinet stood against the far wall. The other walls were obscured by pinned-up maps, charts, graphs, diagrams and documents of all sorts and sizes, and one framed oil painting of a fox hunt which was covered with a dark patina of grime and neglect. The windows had heavy curtains over them, which were drawn closed. The room was brightly lit by three fixtures that depended from the ceiling. I observed them to be electrical lamps with great metallic filaments in evacuated bulbs. This explained the humming noise I had heard: this house had its own electrical generating plant.

Three men were waiting in the room as

we entered: two seated at the table looking stern, and the third pacing about the room with his hands linked behind his back. One of the seated men, a slender, impeccably-dressed, graying man with mutton-chop whiskers, I recognized instantly as Lord Easthope, who holds the post of Foreign Minister in Her Majesty's present Tory government.

'Come, sit down,' said Mycroft Holmes. 'Here they are, gentlemen,' he added, addressing the three men in the room. 'My brother, Sherlock, and Professor James Moriarty.'

The pacing man paused. 'Have they agreed?' he asked.

'No, your lordship. I have not as yet explained the situation to them.'

The third man peered at us over the top of his tortoise-shell glasses. 'So these are the miracle men,' he said.

'Come now, sir,' Mycroft Holmes protested. 'I never claimed that they were miracle men.'

'They'd better be,' the man said.

I took a seat on the right-hand side of the table. Holmes crossed over to the left side and sat where he could keep me in sight while speaking with our hosts.

Mycroft laced his hands behind his back and leaned forward. 'Gentlemen,' he said, addressing Holmes and me, 'may I present their lordships, Lord Easthope and Lord Famm.' (That's the way the name is pronounced. I later learned that His Lordship was Evan Fotheringham, Earl of Stomshire.) 'And His Excellency, Baron van Durm.'

Lord Fotheringham, the gentleman who was pacing the floor, was a tall man with an aristocratic nose and thinning hair. Baron van Durm was a great bear of a man, with heavy, black mutton-chop whiskers and glowering dark eyes. He was impeccably dressed in a pearl-gray morning suit, with a diamond stickpin the size of a robin's egg holding down his white silk cravat.

'I see you have recognized Lord Easthope,' Mycroft said to Holmes and me, reading more from a slight widening of our eyes than most people could from the twenty eight pages of their evening newspaper. 'Lord Fotheringham is Chairman of the Royal Committee for the

Defense of the Realm, and Baron van Durm is General Manager of the Amsterdam branch of the House of van Durm.'

Although the name is not generally recognized outside of government or financial circles, the House of van Durm is one of the richest, most powerful, and most successful private banking houses in the world. With branches in every place you would imagine, and many that would not occur to you, the van Durms have supported governments in need, and brought about the ruin of governments whose policies offended them.

Van Durm nodded his massive head slightly in our direction. Lord Fotheringham paused in his pacing long enough to glower at Sherlock Holmes, Lord Easthope growled a soft monosyllabic growl.

'They know who you are,' Mycroft told us, 'and we, collectively, have something to, ah, discuss with you of the utmost importance, delicacy, and secrecy. Before we continue, I must have your word that nothing we say here will be repeated outside this room.'

I raised an eyebrow. Sherlock looked astonished. 'You have my word,' I said.

'You would trust that — ' Holmes began, pointing a quavering finger at me. Then he paused as Mycroft glared at him, dropped the finger and sighed deeply. 'Oh, very well,' he said. 'You have my word also.'

Mycroft sat down. Lord Fotheringham stopped pacing and stood facing us, arms behind his back. 'Here is the situation, gentlemen,' said his lordship. 'The enemies of Britain are hatching a devilish plot, and there is danger for the safety of this realm — perhaps of the entire world — lurking in every corner of Europe. Plainly put, there is a shadow growing over the British Empire.'

'What is this devilish plot?' I asked.

Lord Easthope focused his mild blue eyes on me. 'There's the heart of the problem,' he said, nodding approvingly, as though I'd said something clever. 'We don't know.'

'A shadow?' Holmes's eyes narrowed. The three noblemen might have thought that he was concentrating his attention on this growing shadow, but I — and probably his brother — knew that he was considering whether Lord Fotheringham should be forcibly restrained. I had some such notion myself.

Holmes leaned back in his chair, his fingers laced over his waistcoat, his eyes almost closed. 'You don't know?'

'Perhaps I should explain,' said Baron van Durm. 'There are signs, subtle but distinct signs, all over Europe, that something of great import is going to happen soon, that it concerns Great Britain, and that it portends no good. Taken by themselves, each of these incidents — these signs — could be a random happening, meaning nothing, but when one looks at them all together a pattern emerges.'

'We have a saying at the War Ministry, Lord Fotheringham interjected. ''Once is happenstance, twice is coincidence, three times is enemy action.'''

Sherlock Holmes leaned forward and laced his hands together beneath his chin, his elbows resting on the table. 'What sort of incidents?' he asked.

Lord Easthope began: 'In various centers of Socialist and Anarchist thought throughout Europe; Paris, Vienna, Prague, speakers have begun warning against British imperialism and the 'secret plans' Britain has for world domination.'

'I see,' I said. ''The Secret Protocols of the Elders of Downing Street,' eh? There is, I grant you, a school of thought that believes that the English are one of the Lost Tribes of Israel.'

'By itself it would be amusing, and hardly sinister,' Easthope said. 'But if you consider these speakers to be part of a plan to pave the way for — something — then they deserve to be looked at more seriously.'

'Even so,' Lord Fotheringham agreed. 'Most of those who listen to this nonsense now, even among the émigré Socialist communities must realize it to be nonsense, considering that Britain is one of the few countries that allows these groups freedom of movement and association without having to worry about police spies in their midst.'

'Unless, of course, they're Irish,'

Mycroft Holmes said bluntly, shifting his bulk forward in his chair. This was met with a complete silence, and he didn't pursue the thought.

'What else?' asked Holmes.

'Newspapers,' said Lord Fotheringham. 'The editorial pages of newspapers in various European countries; France, Germany, Austria, Switzerland, are printing the occasional scurrilous editorial accusing Her Majesty's government of a secret plan of aggression against the continental powers,' Mycroft explained.

'How odd,' said Sherlock.

'We know of three different men in the governments of three different countries who are preparing anti-British legislation of one sort or another,' said Lord Easthope. 'Preparing, you will notice, but not submitting. They are waiting for the proper moment. We must assume that they believe that there soon will be a proper moment. If we know of three, presumably there are more.'

'Do those three men know each other?' Holmes asked.

'Apparently not,' his brother told him.

'Then we must also assume there is, somewhere, a hand pulling the strings.'

'We do so assume,' Mycroft said.

'Is that all?' Holmes asked.

'Is that not enough?' asked Easthope.

'Actually,' said Baron van Durm, 'there is one other thing. The House of van Durm, as you might surmise, has agents strategically placed all over Europe. Most of these conduct the bank's business. Some merely collect information. The success of an international bank rises or falls on the quality of the information it gathers. One of these agents is highly placed in the government of, let us say, a foreign power that has not always been in the best of terms with Great Britain. In the course of his work for us he came across a document, which might shed some light on these happenings. It was not addressed to him.'

'Ah!' said Sherlock Holmes.

'This is a copy of it, translated into English,' van Durm said, removing a sheet of paper from a folder on the table before him and passing it over to Holmes, who read it carefully twice before passing it on to me:

Thirteen —
Your concise and with information filled report was most welcome. We must continue and increase our efforts to discredit England and all things English. It is simpler to chop down a tree if you have poisoned the roots.

Sixteen has failed us. Worse, he may have betrayed us. He was seen entering the embassy on *Prinz Rupert Strasse*. He stayed for an hour. He will not do so again.

The day nears. The events unfold. Work and diligence carry great rewards. The Florida is now ours. Inform the brothers that the direction is up and the peak is in view. If we succeed, we will succeed together. Those who fail will fail alone. It is the time for cleverness and impudence. Stories must be told. Incidents must be arranged.

The lion sleeps peacefully. Holmes and Moriarty are watched, as are Lamphier in Paris and Ettin in Berlin. They are not alert.

Proceed to Lindau on the 16th. The company is assembling. The first place. Three white clothespins. Burn this.
One

'What do you make of that?' asked van Durm.

'It was in German originally?' I asked.

'That is so,' van Durm said.

'The embassy on Prinz Rupert Strasse?'

'The British Embassy in Vienna is on Prinz Rupert Strasse,' Lord Easthope said.

Holmes leaned back in his chair. 'Lindau is a German place-name?' He asked.

'A town on the Bodensee, on the German side of the Austrian border.' Easthope told him.

'Quite a distance from Florida,' Holmes remarked.

'That is so,' Easthope agreed. 'We have not been able to come up with a plausible explanation of that line. Not even, if it comes to that, a fanciful one.'

'The whole missive has something of the fanciful about it,' I said. 'Addressed to

'Thirteen' from 'One.' There's something of the Lewis Carroll about it.'

'Why was it not burned?' asked Holmes.

'It was,' van Drum told him. 'At least the attempt was made. The original was found in a fireplace grate, charred and singed. But it had been folded over several times, and so it was merely the edges that suffered the damage, and the whole message was retrieved intact.'

I smiled, reflecting on the image of a high government official crawling about in a fireplace.

Holmes glared at me. 'I detect your hand in this,' he said.

I was not amused, and I'm afraid that I allowed an ill-considered expletive to pass my lips.

'Quite so,' said Lord Easthope.

'His name is on the document,' Holmes insisted. 'Can't you see — '

'Enough!' cried Mycroft in a deceptively quiet bellow. 'Your name is also on the document. Take my word for it, Sherlock, that whatever else Moriarty may be involved in, he has no hand in these events.'

Sherlock Holmes gave his brother a long glare, and then assumed an attitude of sulky acquiescence from the depths of his chair.

Baron van Durm looked from one to the other of us. 'I thought you said they could work together,' he said to Mycroft.

'They can,' Mycroft assured him. 'They just need a little time to get over their mutual spitting match.'

I resented that. I had done nothing to encourage Holmes in his asinine accusations. But I held my tongue.

'When we saw the references to you, we naturally checked,' Lord Easthope said, 'and ascertained that you were, indeed, being watched. Had you noticed?'

'I assumed that it was at the behest of the younger Mr. Holmes,' I said.

'I thought Moriarty was up to more of his usual deviltry,' snarled Holmes.

'Well there, you see, you were both mistaken,' said Easthope. He turned to Mycroft. 'Are you sure these are the men we want?'

'Yes,' said Mycroft.

'What of Lamphier and Ettin?' Holmes asked.

'Ah!' said van Durm.

'Would that be Alphonse Lamphier the noted French criminologist?' I asked.

'Yes, it would,' van Durm affirmed.

'How can you be sure that he is the Lamphier referred to?' Holmes asked.

'Because he was murdered yesterday.'

'Coincidence,' said Holmes.

'He was found in the ruins of a burned-out cottage outside the village of Lindau,' said Lord Easthope. 'Pure accident that he was found. He — his body — could have stayed there for months. He was almost naked and had his hands tied together. He was already dead when the place was set on fire, but a section of interior wall collapsed and preserved his body from the fire.'

Holmes opened his mouth to say something, but Lord Easthope continued, 'He had scratched some words on his inner thigh with a pin before he died. *Ils se réunissent*. Means 'they meet,' or 'they assemble,' or 'they gather,' depending.'

'I stand corrected,' said Holmes. 'One

can stretch coincidence too far. Does anyone know precisely what he was working on when he was killed?'

'Our agents in Paris are attempting to ascertain that even now,' van Durm said.

'What would you have us do?' I asked.

'As they — whoever they are — are watching you,' said Lord Easthope, 'we infer that they have reason to fear you. Perhaps because of your known abilities, each of you in his own sphere, or perhaps because you possess some information that you might not even know you have, that would be of value.'

Holmes and I pondered this for a minute. Just as I was about to disagree with this diagnosis, Holmes anticipated me. 'I think not,' he said.

'Baron van Durm looked startled. 'Why not?' he asked.

'In Welsh coal mines the miners take a canary down into the pits with them,' Holmes said. 'It is to give them early notice of bad air, as the canaries are more susceptible than the miners. We are these people's canaries.'

'I fail to see the analogy,' said Lord Easthope.

'Our, ah, opponents watch us because they believe that, if Her Majesty's government were to become aware of their machinations, it would send one of us to investigate. Either myself, for obvious reasons, or Professor Moriarty,' he paused for a second to glare at me, and then went on, 'because of his known associations with the underworld of Europe. So much is undoubtedly so. But they no more fear us than the coal miner fears the canary.' Holmes punctuated his talk with restless motions of his slender hands. 'If they believe we have knowledge of their doings, they will immediately and ruthlessly eliminate us.'

'How do you know this, if you know nothing about them?' Lord Fotheringham asked.

'Alphonse Lamphier told me,' Holmes replied.

'What? How could — oh, I see.'

'Perhaps I should have said attempt to eliminate us,' Holmes continued, 'since others have tried, and none have yet succeeded.'

I was amused at Holmes's inclusion of me in his statement, as he had so often accused me of trying to eliminate him. But I said nothing.

'So what are we to do?' asked Baron van Durm.

'Out of the myriad of possibilities,' said Mycroft, 'there are three that appeal more than the others.'

'And they are?' asked Lord Easthope.

'One is to keep my brother and Professor Moriarty visibly at home, to reassure our antagonists, while using others to subvert their plans.'

'Who?' asked Lord Easthope.

'What others?' echoed Baron van Durm.

'I have no idea,' confessed Mycroft Holmes. 'The second possibility is to spirit Holmes and Moriarty away without letting the watchers know.'

'How?' asked Lord Fotheringham.

'Perhaps with wax dummies of the two placed in their windows and moved about to achieve a verisimilitude of life.'

'Ridiculous!' said Baron van Durm.

'The third possibility,' said Mycroft, 'is for them to leave openly, but in such a fashion as to cause those watching them to conclude that their interest are elsewhere.'

Sherlock looked at his brother. 'Brilliant, Mycroft,' he said. 'And just how are we to achieve that?'

The possibilities of the situation appealed to me. 'I'd suggest, Holmes, that you chase me to the ends of the earth, as you've so often threatened to do,' I said, smiling.

Holmes glared at me.

'Perhaps,' Mycroft said, 'with a little modification, that is indeed what we should do.' He rubbed his right forefinger along the side of his nose. 'If the two of you were to kill each other, nobody who knew you would be surprised. And I think it safe to assume that the watchers would cease watching in that event.'

'Kill each other?' Holmes repeated incredulously.

'How do you propose they do that?' asked Baron van Durm.

Mycroft shrugged. 'Somehow and someplace where there can be no suggestion that it was a sham,' he said. 'Plunging over the side of a tall building together would suffice. Perhaps the Eiffel Tower.'

Now this was being carried a bit too far. 'And how do you propose we survive the fall?' I asked.

Mycroft sighed. 'I suppose it should be somewhere less public,' he said, 'so you don't really have to go over the edge.' He sounded honestly regretful. Which of us was he picturing leaping off a precipice, I wondered.

Baron van Durm snapped his fingers. 'I know just the place!' he said.

'Near the town of Meiringen in Switzerland there is a great waterfall on the Reichenbach river.'

'Reichenbach?' asked Holmes.

'A tributary of the Aar,' van Durm explained. 'This spot has but one path leading out to it, and if you were said to have fallen, nobody would expect to find your remains. The river at that point is rapid, deep, and, er, punishing.'

'Why so far from home?' asked Lord Fotheringham.

'It has several advantages,' said Holmes

thoughtfully. 'Our trip there will give our opponents time to see that we are chasing each other rather than hunting for them, and it will leave us in Switzerland, and a lot closer to Germany and the village of Lindau.'

'Even so,' Mycroft agreed.

'Won't that make them suspicious, your ending up in Switzerland?' Lord Easthope asked.

I ventured a reply. 'They know nothing of our interest in Lindau, and if they believe us dead, it won't matter anyway.'

'That is so,' Easthope agreed.

'So,' said Lord Fotheringham. 'Do you two gentlemen believe that you can put your personal enmity aside long enough to serve your queen?'

I was about to answer with a polite guffaw, or perhaps even a mild snicker, when to my surprise Holmes stood up and drew his shoulders back. 'For queen and country,' he said.

All eyes were at that instant on me. I shrugged. 'I have nothing on for the next few weeks,' I said.

With a slight change in the original plan, the race across Europe was to be carried out with a verisimilitude designed to convince Watson, as well as any onlookers, that it was genuine. The change was that I was to pursue Holmes rather than the other way around. Mycroft decided that would be more convincing.

Two days later the great chase began. Holmes called upon Watson to tell him that I was trying to kill him (Holmes), and he must flee to Europe. The tale was that my 'gang' was about to be rounded up by the police, but until that was accomplished Holmes was in great danger. Watson agreed to accompany him in his flight, and the next day joined Holmes in 'the second first-class carriage from the front' of the Continental Express at Victoria Station. Holmes was disguised as a humble elderly prelate, but Watson wore no disguise, and so the watchers had no trouble watching. They saw Holmes and Watson flee in the Express, and watched me engage a

Special Train to pursue them. Holmes and Watson appeared to elude me by abandoning their luggage and getting off the Express at Canterbury. They went cross-country to Newhaven, and thence by the paddle steamer *Brittany* to Dieppe.

Shaking my fist and murmuring 'Curses, foiled again!,' I went straight through to Paris and lingered about their luggage for several days, apparently waiting for them to come and claim it. When they didn't show I put the word out among the European underworld that I would pay a substantial reward for information as to the whereabouts of two Englishmen who looked thus-and-so. Eventually word came to me, and I spent several days pursuing them about Europe, followed in turn by several gentlemen who did their best to stay just out of sight.

As planned, I caught up with Holmes and Watson in the village of Meiringen in Switzerland on May 6th. They had gone after lunch to look at the falls, about a two-hour hike away from the inn, and I sent a boy with a note to Watson designed to lure him back to the inn to care for a mythical sick woman. Holmes was then to write a letter to Watson, put it and some article of clothing on the ledge, and disappear; leaving it to be believed that he and I had gone over the edge in a mighty battle of good and evil. Humph! I would then fade away from the scene and meet Holmes in Lindau in four days.

But it was not to be. Even as the lad scurried off to carry the note to Watson, I was forced to change the plan. I followed and concealed myself behind a boulder when I saw the lad and Watson hurrying back. Then I rushed forward to the ledge, where Holmes had already put the note in his silver cigarette-box, placed it by his alpenstock at the side of a rock, and was enjoying one last pipe of that foul tobacco he smokes before disappearing.

'Aha!' he said, upon spying me approach. 'I knew it was too good to be true! So it's to be an all-out fight to the death, is it professor?' He sprang to his feet and grabbed for the alpenstock.

'Don't speak nonsense, Holmes,' I growled. 'One of the men following us reached the inn just as I sent the lad off with the note. If I didn't come after you while he watched, he couldn't possibly be convinced that we both plunged off the cliff.'

'So!' said Holmes. 'It seems we must fight after all, or at least leave behind convincing marks of a scuffle, and perhaps a few bits of tattered clothing.'

'And then we must find some way to leave this ledge without going back the way we came. Two sets of footprints returning on the path would give the game away.' I walked over to the edge and looked down. The way was sheer, and steep, and in some places the rock face appeared to be undercut, so that it would be impossible to climb down without pitons and ropes and a variety of other mountaineering gear that we had neglected to bring. 'We can't go down,' I said.

'Well then,' Holmes said briskly, 'we must go up.'

I examined the cliff face behind us. 'Possible,' I concluded. 'Difficult, but possible.'

'But first we must scuff up the ground by the cliff edge in a convincing manner,' said Holmes.

'Let us run through the third and fourth Baritsu katas,' I suggested. I took off my inverness and put it and my owl-headed walking stick and hat on a nearby outcropping and assumed the first, or 'waiting crab' Baritsu defensive position.

Holmes responded by taking off his hat and coat. 'We must be careful not to kill each other by accident,' he said. 'I should hate to kill you by accident.'

'And I, you,' I assured him.

We ran through the martial exercises for about a quarter-hour, getting ourselves and the ground quite scuffed up in the process. 'Enough!' Holmes said finally.

'I agree,' I said. 'One last touch.' I took my stick from the rock and gave the handle a quarter turn, releasing the 8-inch blade concealed within. 'I hate to do this,' I said, 'but in the interest of verisimilitude . . . '

Holmes eyes me warily while I rolled

up my right sleeve and carefully stabbed my arm with the sharp point of the blade. I smeared the last few inches of the blade liberally with my own blood, and then threw the weapon aside as though it had been lost in combat. The shaft of the stick I left by the rock. 'For queen and country,' I said, wrapping my handkerchief around the cut and rolling down my sleeve.

'Left handed, are you?' Holmes asked. 'I should have guessed.'

We retrieved the rest of our clothing and began climbing the almost-sheer face of the cliff above us. It was slow, tedious work, made more dangerous by the fact that it was already late afternoon, and the long shadows cast across the chasm made it difficult to see clearly.

After about twenty minutes, Holmes who, despite a constant stream of muttered complaints, had been clambering up the cliff side with great energy, and was about two body lengths above me, cried out, 'Aha! Here is a shelf big enough to hold us! Perhaps we should rest here.'

I scrambled up beside him, and the two

of us lay on the moss-covered rock shelf with just our heads showing over the edge as we peered down into the gathering dusk below. We were, I estimate, some two hundred feet above the ledge we had left.

I'm not sure how long we lay there, as it was too dark to read the face of my pocket watch and we dare not strike a light. But after some time we could make out somebody coming onto the ledge we had recently deserted. He was carrying a small lantern, in the light of which he proceeded to make a minute study of the earth, the surrounding rocks, and the cliff face both above and below the ledge, although he didn't cast the beam high enough to see us where we were peering down at him. After a minute he found the cigarette box that Holmes had left for Watson, and he carefully opened it, read the note inside, then closed it again and replaced it on the rock. Another minute's searching brought him to the bloodied blade, which he peered at closely, tested with his finger, and then secured under his coat. Then he slowly went back the way he had come, closely examining the footprints on the path as he went.

About ten minutes later we heard voices below, and four men approached the cliff edge: two Swiss men from the inn in their green lederhosen, carrying large bright lanterns; Dr. Watson, and the man who had recently left. 'No,' the man was saying as they came into view, 'I saw no one on the trail. I do not know what happened to your friend.'

Watson wandered about the cliff, looking here and there without really knowing what he was looking at, or for. 'Holmes!' he cried. 'My God, Holmes, where are you?'

Holmes stirred next to me and seemed about to say something, but he refrained.

One of the Swiss men spotted the silver cigarette box. 'Is that a belonging of your friend?' he asked, pointing to it.

Watson rushed over to it. 'Yes!' he said. 'That is Holmes's.' He turned it over in his hand. 'But why — ' Opening the box, he pulled out the letter, tearing it halfway down the middle in the process. 'Moriarty!' he said, reading the letter by the light of one of the lanterns. 'Then it has happened. It is as I feared.' He folded the letter and put it in his pocket, and went over to the edge of the cliff to peer down into the inky blackness below. 'Goodbye, my friend,' he said, his voice choked with emotion. 'The best and finest man I have ever known.' Then he turned to the others. 'Come,' he said, 'we can do no good here.'

* * *

As we were unable to safely climb down in the dark, Holmes and I spent the night on that rock shelf, our greatcoats offering what protection they could from the chill wind. Shortly before dawn a cold rain fell, and we were drenched and chilled before first light, when we were finally able to make our way back down to the ledge below. We traveled overland on foot, with an occasional ride on the ox cart of a friendly farmer, for the next two days until we reached Wurstheim, where we settled into the Wurstheimer Hof, bathed, slept for twelve hours, bought suitable clothing, and altered our appearance. The next morning I went down to a stationer's and procured some drafting supplies, and then spent a few hours in my room creating a few useful documents. Leaving Wurstheim late that afternoon were a French officer of Artillery in mufti — Holmes speaks fluent French, having spent several years in Montpellier during his youth, and makes quite a dashing officer of Artillery — and a German Senior Inspector of Canals and Waterworks. I have no idea whether there actually is such a position, but the papers I drew up looked quite authentic. I also crafted one more document that I thought might be useful.

'The world lost a master forger when you decided to become a, ah, professor of mathematics, Moriarty,' Holmes told me, looking over the papers I had produced with a critical eye. 'The watermarks would give the game away, if anyone is astute enough to examine them, but you've done a very creditable job.'

'Praise from the master is praise indeed,' I told him.

He looked at me suspiciously, but then folded up the *laisser-passer* I had created for him and thrust it into an inner pocket.

In the early afternoon of the 14th of May we arrived in Kreuzingen, a small town on the east shore of Lake Constance, or as the Germans call it, Bodensee — a great swelling in the river Rhine some 40 miles long and, in places, ten miles wide. It is where Switzerland, Germany, and Austria meet, or would meet if there weren't a lake in the way. We boarded the paddle steamer *König Freidrich* for the four-hour trip across to Lindau, a quiet resort town on the German side of the lake. Holmes, as *Le Commandant* Martin Vernet of the *Corps d'Artillerie*, had his hair parted in the middle and severely brushed down on both sides and sported a quite creditable brush mustache. He wore a severely-tailored gray suit with the miniature ribbon of a *Chevalier* of the *Légion d'Honneur* in his button-hole, and cultivated a slight limp. He would effect a complete lack of knowledge of either German or English, and thus stood a good chance of overhearing things he was not meant to overhear.

I became Herr Inspektor Otto Stuhl of the *Büro des Direktors der Kanäle und des Wasserversorgung*, and thus could be expected to take an interest in water and all things wet, which gave me a plausible reason to poke around in places where I had no business poking around.

We amused ourselves on the trip across by discerning the professions of our fellow passengers. The Swiss, like the Germans, make the task simpler by dressing strictly according to their class, status and occupation. We disagreed over a pair of gentlemen with ruffled shirts and double rows of brass buttons going down their overly-decorated lederhosen. I guessed them to be buskers of some sort, while Holmes thought them hotel tour guides. On overhearing their conversation, we determined them to be journeymen plumbers. Holmes glared at me as though it were somehow my fault.

We took rooms at the Hotel Athènes, carefully not knowing each other as we checked in. There would have been some advantage in taking rooms in separate hotels, but the difficulty in sharing information without being noticed would have been too great. Holmes, or rather Vernet, was to go around to the inns and spas in the area and discover which ones had public rooms where a group might gather, or more probably large private rooms for rent, and listen to the conversation of the guests. Stuhl would speak to various town officials about the very important subject of water, and partake of such gossip as they might offer. Town officials love to pass on tit-bits of important sounding gossip to passing government bureaucrats; it reaffirms their authority.

'Three white clothespins,' Holmes mused, staring out the window at one of the great snow-capped mountains that glowered down at the town. It was the morning of the 15th, and we had just come up from our separate breakfasts and were meeting in my room on the third floor of the hotel. Holmes's room was down the hall and across the way, and had a view across the town square to the police station, and then the lake beyond. My window overlooked only mountains.

'The last line of that letter,' I remembered. ''Proceed to Lindau on the Sixteenth. The company is assembling. The first place. Three white clothespins. Burn this.' Very terse.'

'The first place implies there was a second place,' Holmes mused. 'So it would seem they have met here before.'

'More than that,' I offered, 'one of their leaders probably lives around here.'

'Perhaps,' Holmes agreed. 'Consider: If the company is 'assembling,' then they are gathering in order to do whatever it is they are preparing to do. If they were merely coming together to discuss matters, or to receive instructions, then they would be meeting, not assembling. The study of language and its connotations holds great value for the serious investigator.'

'Even so,' I agreed.

Holmes — Vernet — went out that day and passed from inn to café to public house, and drank cassis and coffee and ate pastries. The man has an amazing ability to eat and eat without gaining weight and, conversely, to go without food for days at a time when on the track of a miscreant. I spent the morning studying a map of the town, to get a sense of where things were. After lunch I went to the town hall to see Herr Bürgermeister Pindl, a large man in many directions with a massive mustache and a smile that spread broadly across his face and radiated good cheer. We sat in his office and he poured us each a small glass of schnapps, and we discussed matters of water supply and public health. He seemed quite pleased that the great bureaucracy in far-off Berlin would even know of the existence of little Lindau.

If you would impress a man with your insight, tell him that you sense that he is worried about a relationship, about his finances, or about his health. Better, tell him that he fears — justly — that he is often misunderstood, and that his work is not appreciated. If you would impress a civic official, tell him that you share his concern about the town's water supply, its sewage, or its garbage. Within the first ten minutes of our conversation, Herr Pindl and I had been friends for years. But the smiling giant was not as simple as he appeared. 'Tell me,' he said, holding his schnapps daintily in two chubby fingers, 'what does the ministry really want to know? You're not just here to see if the water is coming out of the faucets.'

I beamed at him as a professor beams at his best pupil. 'You're very astute,' I said, leaning toward him. 'And you look like a man who can keep a secret . . . '

'Oh, I am,' he assured me, his nose twitching like that of a stout bird dog on the scent of a blutwurst sausage.

Extracting my very special document from an inner pocket, I unfolded it before him. Crowded with official-looking seals and imperial eagles, the paper identified Otto Stuhl as an officer in the *Nachrichtendienst*, the Kaiser's Military Intelligence Service, holding the rank of Oberst, and further declared:

His Imperial Most-High Excellency Kaiser Wilhelm II requests and demands all loyal German subjects to give the bearer of this document whatever assistance he requires at all times.

'Ah!' said Bürgermeister Pindl, nodding ponderously. 'I have heard of such things.'

Thank God, I thought, that you've never seen one before, since I have no idea what a real one looks like.

'Well, Herr Oberst Stuhl,' Pindl asked, 'what can the Bürgermeister of Lindau do for you?'

I took a sip of schnapps. It had a strong, peppery taste. 'Word has come,' I said, 'of certain unusual activities in this area. I have been sent to investigate.'

'Unusual?'

I nodded. 'Out of the ordinary.'

A look of panic came into his eyes. 'I assure you, Herr Oberst, that we have done nothing — '

'No, no,' I assured him, wondering what illicit activity he and his *kameraden* had been indulging in. Another time it might have been interesting to find out. 'We of the *Nachrichtendienst*, care not what petty offenses local officials may be indulging in — short of treason.' I

131

chuckled. 'You don't indulge in treason, do you?'

We shared a good laugh together about that, although the worried look did not completely vanish from his eyes.

'No, it's strangers I'm concerned with' I told him. 'Outsiders.'

'Outsiders.'

'Just so. We have received reports from our agents that suspicious activities have been happening in this area.'

'What sort of suspicious activities?'

'Ah!' I waggled my finger at him. 'That's what I was hoping *you* would tell *me*.'

He got up and went over to the window. 'It must be those *verdammter* Englanders,' he said, slapping his large hand against his even larger thigh.

'English?' I asked. 'You are, perhaps, infested with Englishmen?'

'We have people coming from all the world,' he told me. 'We are a resort. We are on the Bodensee. But recently a group of Englanders has attracted our attention.'

'How?'

'By trying not to attract our attention, if you see what I mean. First, they come separately and pretend not to know each other. But they are seen talking — whispering — together by the twos and threes.'

'Ah!' I said. 'Whispering. That is most interesting.'

'And then they all go boating,' the Bürgermeister said.

'Boating?'

'Yes. Separately, by ones and twos, they rent or borrow boats and row, paddle, or sail out onto the Bodensee. Sometimes they come home in the evening, sometimes they don't.'

'Where do they go?'

'I don't know,' Pindl said. 'We haven't followed them.'

'How long has this been going on?' I asked.

'Off and on, for about a year,' he said. 'They go away for a while, and then they come back. Which is another reason we noticed them. The same collection of Englanders who don't know each other appearing at the same time every few months. Really!'

'How many of them would you say there were?' I asked.

'Perhaps two dozen,' he said. 'Perhaps more.'

I thought this over for a minute. 'Is there anything else you can tell me about them?' I asked.

He shrugged. 'All ages, all sizes,' he said. 'All men, as far as I know. Some of them speak perfect German. Some, I've been told, speak fluent French. They all speak English.'

I stood up. 'Thank you,' I said. 'The *Nachrichtendienst* will not forget the help you have been.'

I had dinner at a small waterfront restaurant, and watched the shadows grow across the lake as the sun sank behind the mountains. After dinner I returned to my room, where Holmes joined me about an hour later.

I related my experiences of the day, and he nodded thoughtfully and went 'hmmm' twice. 'Englanders,' he said. 'Interesting. I think the game's afoot.'

'What game are we stalking, Holmes?' I asked.

'I have seen some of your 'Englanders,'' he told me. 'In the Ludwig Hof shortly after lunch. I was enjoying a cassis and being expansively French when three men walked in and sat near me. They tried to engage me in conversation in English and German and, when I effected not to understand, bad French. We exchanged a few pleasantries and they tipped their hats and began speaking among themselves in English, which, incidentally, is not as good as their German.'

'Ah!' I said.

'They insulted me several times in English, commenting with little imagination on my appearance and my probable parentage, and when I didn't respond they became convinced that I couldn't understand and thereafter spoke freely.'

'Saying?'

'Well, one thing that will interest you, is that Holmes and Moriarty are dead.'

'Really? And how did they die?'

'There was this great fight at Reichenbach Falls, and they both plunged in. Their correspondent saw it happen himself. There could be no mistake.'

I stared out the window at the snow covering a distant mountain peak. 'Oscar Wilde says that people who are said to be dead often turn up later in San Francisco,' I said. 'I've never been to San Francisco.'

Holmes stared intently down his long nose at me. 'I don't know what to make of you,' he said. 'I never have.'

'So, now that we're officially dead,' I said, 'what do we do next?'

'When the faux Englishmen left the room,' Holmes continued. 'I followed them. They went to the waterfront.'

'I trust you were not seen,' I said.

Holmes fastened a withering glare on the painting of an alpine meadow on the far wall. 'When I don't wish to be seen,' he stated, 'I am not seen.'

'Silly of me,' I said. 'What did you observe?'

'They entered a large warehouse next to a pier jutting into the lake. Attached to a short line by the warehouse door — '

'Three clothespins,' I ventured.

'Three *white* clothespins,' he corrected.

'Well,' I said. 'Now we know where.'

'Not quite,' Holmes said. 'I observed several more people entering the warehouse over the next hour. And then a door opened on the water side of the building, and the men boarded a steam launch named the *Isolde*, which was tied up to the pier next to the building. It then chuffed out onto the lake and away. I investigated and discovered that now there was only one man, an old caretaker, left in the warehouse.'

'Ah!' I said.

'The boat returned about an hour ago. Some men got off. A few of them were the same men who had boarded earlier, but not all.' he tapped his long, thin forefinger on the table. 'They're doing something out there somewhere on the lake. But it's a big lake.'

'That presents an interesting problem,' I said. 'How do we follow them over open water?'

Holmes stared out the window. 'A two-pipe problem,' he said, pulling out his ancient brier and stuffing it with tobacco. 'Perhaps three.'

Having smelled the foul mixture he prefers to smoke, I excused myself and went downstairs, where I indulged in a *kaffee mit schlag. Mit*, as it happens, extra *schlag*. About an hour later Holmes came downstairs, gave a slight nod in my direction and went out the front door. After a suitable time I followed. Night had fallen, and the streetlights were sparse and dim. A chill wind was blowing in off the lake.

Holmes was standing in the shadow of an old stable a block away. I smelled the foul tobacco odor emanating from his clothing before I actually saw him.

'Commandant Vernet,' I said.

'Herr Stuhl.'

'Have your three pipes shown the way?'

'If we had time we could build a large observation balloon and watch them from high aloft,' Holmes said. 'But we have no time. I think one of us will have to stow away on that steam launch and see where she goes.'

'If nominated I shall not run,' I told him firmly, 'and if elected I shall not serve.'

'What's that?'

'The American General Sherman. I am taking his excellent advice.'

Holmes looked at me with distaste. 'With all your faults,' he said, 'I didn't picture you as a coward.'

'And neither am I foolhardy,' I told him. 'There is little point in indulging in a foredoomed course of action when it will accomplish nothing and merely succeed in getting one killed. Remember Alphonse Lamphier.'

Holmes stared glumly into the dark. 'I have nothing better to offer,' he said. 'In large parts of the ocean ships leave a phosphorescent wake that lasts for some time, I understand, but not in lakes, however large.'

'What an excellent idea!' I said.

'A phosphorescent wake?'

'A wake of some sort. The craft will go wherever it is to go, and we shall follow in its wake.'

'How?'

'A moment,' I said, staring into space. 'Why not oil? Some light oil dyed red should do it.'

'Brilliant!' said Holmes. 'And who shall we get to sprinkle this oil on the water as the boat progresses?'

'We, my doubting Sherlock, shall construct a mechanism to do the task,' I said.

And so we did. The next morning I procured a five-gallon drum of fish oil, which seemed appropriate, and took it down to a deserted jetty which Holmes had observed yesterday in his wanderings. I then went back to the main street and returned with a pair of iron exercise dumbbells, purchased from a junk shop. Holmes joined me shortly after, bringing a coil of quarter-inch marine line and a small bottle of red dye; some sort of pastry dye I believe, which we added to the oil. It seemed to mix satisfactorily, so we busied ourselves affixing some handles on the drum with metal screws. The screw holes would leak slightly, but that didn't matter.

We changed into recently purchased bathing costumes and rented a two-man rowboat, wrapping our clothing and other items we might need in oilcloth and stowing them on the bottom of the small craft. After about twenty minutes rowing along the shore we came in sight of the pier in question. The steam launch *Isolde* was tied up alongside.

There appeared to be no one on watch in the launch, so we came up as quietly as possible to the opposite side of the pier and tied our boat to a convenient hook. Slipping into the chill water, we towed the drum of oil under the pier to the starboard side of the *Isolde*. We could hear the deep chugging of the steam engine as we approached the boat, which suggested that there would shortly be another journey.

I screwed two four-inch wood screws into the hull near the stern, and fastened one end of a twelve-foot length of marine line to them. The other end Holmes fastened to the oil drum. My calculations indicated that it would take the weight of both of the iron dumbbells to keep the drum submerged, so the two of them were tied firmly onto the sides of the drum. All that remained was to put a screw into the cork plugging the drum's bunghole and attach it by a short line to the pier. That way as the steam launch left the pier, the cork would be pulled and the drum would begin leaking colored oil.

As we were completing this last task we heard footsteps above us on the pier, and the voices of the pseudo Englanders as they began boarding the launch. They all spoke English, those who spoke, and their accents were slight. Yet of all the myriad of homegrown accents which pepper the British Isles, allowing one man to despise another who grew up twenty miles to his north, these were none.

After about ten minutes the boarding was completed, the chugging of the steam engine grew louder and deeper, and the *Isolde* pulled away from the pier. There was a slight but satisfying *pop* as the cork was pulled from the oil drum, and it began its journey bobbing out of sight behind the steam launch, spilling red oil as it went.

'We'd better get out of the water,' said Holmes, 'I'm losing sensation in my hands and feet.'

'Cold baths are much over-rated,' I

agreed, shivering uncontrollably as I threw myself back into the rowboat. I held it steady for Holmes to climb aboard, and then we were both occupied for some time in toweling ourselves off and putting our garments back on.

'Let's get going,' Holmes said after a few minutes. 'They're getting further ahead by the moment, and besides the exercise of rowing will warm us up.'

I took up one pair of oars, and Holmes the other, and we maneuvered our small craft out onto the lake. The sun was overhead, and a slight but clearly visible red stain was slowly widening as it led off in the direction of the departing steam launch, which was already distant enough for its image to be covered by my thumb with my arm extended.

We rowed energetically after the *Isolde*, cutting easily through the gentle swells left by her wake. If she was barely visible to us, surely our small craft was no more than a speck to any of her company who should chance to be peering back toward shore. Soon she was out of sight entirely, and we followed by keeping in sight the slight red smear visible under the bright sun.

It was perhaps half an hour later when the tenuous watery red trail brought us in sight of the steam launch. She was headed back toward us, pulling away from a large black barge, which had a curious superstructure, and seemed to have been outfitted with some sort of engine at the rear. At any rate, the barge was moving slowly under its own power even as the *Isolde* pulled away. The deck of the Isolde was crowded with men and, as it seemed probable that there were even more men inside the cabin, it looked as though the crew of the black barge were going home for the night.

We altered our course slightly to make it appear that we were headed for the opposite shore, and tried to look like two middle aged gentlemen who were passionate about rowing, perhaps recapturing their youth. As the *Isolde* approached us we waved in a friendly but disinterested manner, and two of the men on deck replied with similar salutations. Who, I wondered, was fooling whom? I hoped it was us, them, or our story might have quite a different ending than we had intended.

'What now?' Holmes asked me, when it was clear that the steam launch was not going to turn around and investigate us more closely.

'The black barge,' I said.

'Of course,' Holmes told me. 'I repeat, what now?'

'As it's still under power, although making slight headway, there are still men aboard,' I said. 'So just pulling alongside and clambering on deck is probably not a wise option.'

Holmes lifted his oars out of the water and turned to glare at me. 'Astute observation,' he said. 'I repeat, what now?'

'We could swim over to it underwater if the water wasn't so cold; if we could swim that far under water. We could come alongside and flail about, claiming to be in distress, and see whether those aboard choose to rescue us.'

'Or just shoot us and toss us overboard,' Holmes commented.

'Yes, there's always that possibility,' I agreed.

Holmes sighed deeply. 'I guess there's nothing for it then,' he said, shipping the oars and laying back in his seat to stare at the cloud-filled sky. 'We float about here until dark and spend our time praying for it not to rain.'

Which is what we did. Our prayers were almost answered, in that a light, but extremely cold drizzle fell for a while, but then went away to be replaced by a chill wind.

One thing I must say about Holmes is that, barring his periodic fixation on me as the fount of all that is evil, he is a good companion: dependable and steadfast in adversity, intelligent and quick-thinking in a fix; a loyal ally and, as I have had occasion to discover in the past, a formidable foe. I found myself thinking about Holmes and our past history as we waited. What Holmes thought about I cannot say.

Dark fell with admirable speed that evening. By ten past eight I couldn't read my pocket watch without striking a match

— the light well shielded from view, of course. There were no lights visible from the black barge either. If lamps were lit in the cabins, the windows and portholes must have been well shielded. We waited a while longer — how long I cannot say as I didn't want to strike another match — and then, dipping our oars as silently as possible, headed in the direction of the barge. The moon was a slender crescent, the light was scant, and the barge proved as difficult to find as you might imagine a black barge on an almost moonless night would do. For a while we could hear the painfully slow throb of the barge's motor, but it was impossible to tell from just what direction it was coming. And the sound carried so well over the water that it did not seem to increase or lessen in whatever direction we rowed. And then it stopped. It wasn't until a man came on deck carrying a lantern, heading from the aft deckhouse to the forward deckhouse, that we were able to be sure of our heading. In another five minutes we were under the stern overhang of the barge, where we tied the rowboat up to the port side and paused to consider.

'Up onto the deck, find a blunt object or two to use as weapons, and get below, or at least inside, as quickly as possible,' Holmes said.

'Forward or aft?' I asked.

'We are aft,' Holmes said, 'so let us not waste time by going forward.'

I agreed. We moved the rowboat around to the side of the barge as far as we could without untying it and I felt about for a handhold. 'Well!' I whispered. 'Piety and good works are indeed rewarded in this life.'

'What?' Holmes murmured.

'There's a ladder fixed to the side here,' I told him. I took hold with both hands and started up, with Holmes right behind me. Once on deck we moved toward the rear cabin, feeling our way along the railing. I reached some impediment; a large metal object covered with a canvas and gutta-percha weather shield, and paused to feel my way around it and to determine what it was — like the blind man trying to describe an elephant. But after a few moments of grasping and groping the outline of the elephant became clear.

'Well I'll be!' I said, or perhaps it was something stronger.

'What is it?' asked Holmes, who was right behind me.

'It is a three-inch naval gun, probably a Hoskins and Reed. It will fire a nine-pound projectile something over three miles accurately. It's the latest thing in gunnery. Royal Navy destroyers are being outfitted with them even now.'

'I didn't know you were so well acquainted with naval ballistics,' Holmes said. His voice sounded vaguely accusatory, but then it often does when he speaks to me.

'I am well acquainted with a wide range of things,' I told him.

We continued our progress toward the aft deckhouse. I was hoping to come across a belaying pin, or a length of iron pipe, or anything that could be worked loose and used as a weapon, but nothing came to hand.

We reached the deckhouse door and Holmes pulled it open. It was as dark inside as out. We entered. By creeping ahead silently and feeling along the wall we were able to ascertain that we were in a corridor of unknown length, with doors on each side.

Light suddenly cascaded into the corridor as a door further down was opened. A man stood in the doorway talking to someone inside the room, but in another second he would surely come into the corridor. I tugged at Holmes's sleeve and pointed to what the light had just revealed: a stairs, or as they call anything with steps on a ship a ladder, going up. By mounting quickly we could avoid being seen. We did so. There was a door at the head of the ladder, which I opened and we went through. The door made a loud 'click' on closing, and we paused, waiting to see whether this would alert those below. Holmes assumed the 'Standing Locust' Baritsu posture to the left of the door, ready in mind and body for whoever might come through. I grabbed a spanner from a nearby shelf and stood, poised, on the right side.

There were no hurried footsteps up the

ladder, no whispered voices from downstairs, so after a few moments we relaxed and looked around. An oil lamp on gimbals mounted to the ceiling cast a dull light around the room. It appeared to be the wheelhouse of a large vessel, with the forward windows covered with heavy drapes. There was an oversized ship's wheel in the center, with calling pipes, and a ship's telegraph, a chart cabinet and chart table to the rear, and various bits of nautical equipment affixed here and there throughout the room. A captain's chair was bolted to the deck on the left, excuse me, port side, and a ship's compass squatted alongside. A metal-strapped leather chest big enough to hold a fair sized man doubled over sat on the other side of the chair.

'A wheelhouse for a barge,' Holmes whispered. 'How odd.'

'It does have an engine,' I said.

'Yes, but I doubt if it can attain a speed of greater than three or four knots. One would think that a tiller would suffice.' He took the oil lamp off its mount and began a slow inspection of the room, bending, sniffing, peering and probing at the walls, floor, and bits of apparatus scattered about. The chest was securely locked, and there seemed to be nothing else of interest in the room. After a few minutes he stood erect and put the lantern on the chart table. 'This is very peculiar,' he said.

'It is indeed,' I agreed. 'This is not the wheelhouse of a scow — this is the command bridge of a naval ship.'

'Say rather a mockup or model of it,' Holmes said. 'The chart cabinet is devoid of charts, and the chart that's pinned to this table is a Royal Navy chart of the Bay of Naples.'

'Perhaps,' I suggested, 'we have found the fabled Swiss navy.'

'I think not,' Holmes said. 'I found this.' He held out a blue cap for my perusal. It was a British Navy seaman's cap, and on the side the words 'H.M.S. Royal Edgar' were embroidered in gold thread.

'The Royal Edgar is a destroyer,' I told Holmes. 'Royal Henry class. Four funnels. Six torpedo tubes. Two four-inch and eight two-inch guns. Top speed a hair under thirty knots.'

'How do you happen to know that?' Holmes asked, an undercurrent of suspicion creeping into his voice.

'I have recently done some work for the admiralty,' I explained. 'I, of course, made it a point to learn the names and ratings of all of Her Majesty's ships currently in service.'

He shook the cap in my face. 'You mean they trust you to — ' he paused and took a deep breath. 'Never mind,' he finished. He pointed across the room. 'That chest may hold something of import, but the rest of the room is devoid of interest.

'Except for the hat,' I said.

'Yes,' he agreed. 'That is very interesting.'

'I didn't bring my lock picks,' I said, 'and if we break the chest open, we will be announcing our presence.'

'Interesting conundrum,' Holmes allowed.

It was one we never got the chance to resolve. There was a rumbling and a thudding and a screeching and the sound of voices from below. No — from the deck outside. Holmes closed the lantern and we pulled one of the curtains aside to see what was happening.

The steam launch had returned and was now tied up alongside. If the men now embarking from it saw our rowboat tied up at the stern life would get interesting over the next few minutes. But the rowboat had swung back around out of sight, and it would be an unlucky accident if they were to see it.

There was a barking of orders — in German, I noted — and the eight or ten men who had come aboard scurried about to do whatever they had come aboard to do. Three of them headed to the door in the aft deckhouse below us, and the two men inside had opened the door to greet them.

'If they come up here . . . ' Holmes said.

'Yes,' I said, remembering the layout of the darkened room. 'There is no place to conceal ourselves.'

'Behind these curtains is the only possibility,' Holmes whispered. 'And that's not a good one.'

'Well,' I said, hearing the tramp of boots on the ladder,' it will have to do.'

We retreated to the far side of the curtains and twitched them closed scant seconds before I heard the door being opened and two — no, three — sets of footsteps entering the room.

'The lamp must have gone out,' one of them said in German. 'I'll light it.'

'No need,' another replied in the same language, the sound of authority in his voice. 'All we need from here is the chest. Shine your light over there — there. Yes, there it is. You two, pick it up.'

'Yes, Your Grace.'

'Take it down and onto the launch right away,' the imperious voice said. 'This must accompany us on the train to Trieste.'

'Right away, Your Grace.' And, with a minor cacophony of thumps, bumps and groans, the chest was lifted and carried out the door. After a few seconds it was clear that His Grace had left with the chest, and we were once again alone in the room.

'Well,' I said, stepping out from behind

the curtain. 'Trieste. Now if we only knew — '

Holmes held his hand up to silence me. He was peering out of the window with a concentrated fury, glaring down at our recent guests as they went on deck through the downstairs door.

'What is it?' I asked.

'One moment,' he said.

For a second 'his grace' turned his head, and his profile was illuminated by the lantern carried by one of the crew. Holmes staggered backward and clapped his hand to his forehead. 'I was not wrong!' he said. 'I knew I recognized that voice!'

'Who, His Grace?' I asked.

'He!' he said. 'It is he!'

'Whom?'

'His name is Wilhelm Gottsreich Sigismond von Ormstein,' Holmes told me. 'Grand Duke of Cassel-Felstein and Hereditary King of Bohemia.'

'Is he indeed?' I asked. 'And how do you know His Grace?'

'He employed me once,' Holmes said. 'I will not speak of it further.'

'The case had nothing to do with our current, er, problem?' I asked.

'Nothing,' he assured me.

'Then I, also, shall not speak of it again.' Whatever it was, it must have affected Holmes greatly, but now was not the time to pick at old wounds. 'I take it he has little use for the English?' I asked.

'He has little regard for anything British,' Holmes affirmed. 'And I believe that he has no fondness for anyone except himself, and possibly members of his immediate family.'

'Truly a prince,' I said.

The last of our visitors boarded the steam launch, and it cast off and pulled away from the barge. 'I wonder what prompted the midnight visit,' I said.

'Nothing good,' Holmes opined.

There was a crumping sound, as of a distant belching beneath the water, and then another, and the barge listed toward the starboard side with a great creaking and a series of snaps.

'There's your answer,' Holmes said, as we both grabbed for the nearest support in order to remain upright. 'Those were explosions. They're scuttling this craft. She'll be under in ten minutes, unless she breaks apart first, and then it will be faster. Much faster.'

'Perhaps we should make our exit,' I suggested.

'Perhaps,' he agreed.

We hurried down the ladder and onto the deck.

'Hilfe! Hilfen sie mir, bitte!'

The faint cry for help came from somewhere forward. 'We're coming!' I called into the dark. *'Wir kommen! Wo sind Sie?'*

'Ich weiss nicht. In einem dunklen Raum,' came the reply.

' 'In a dark room' doesn't help,' Holmes groused. 'It couldn't be any darker than it is out here.'

The barge picked that moment to lurch and sag further to starboard.

'Hilfe!'

We struggled our way to the forward deckhouse. The cry for help was coming from somewhere to the left of the door. I felt my way along the wall until I came to a porthole. 'Hello!' I called inside, knocking on the glass.

'Oh, thank God,' cried the man in German. 'You have found me! You must, for the love of God, untie me before this wretched vessel sinks.'

Holmes and I went in through the door and down a short length of corridor until we came to a left-hand turn.

'Ow!' said Holmes.

'What?'

I heard a scraping sound. 'Wait a second,' Holmes said. 'I've just banged my head.'

'Sorry,' I said.

'No need,' he told me. 'I've just banged my head on a lantern hanging from the ceiling. Give me a second and I'll have it lit.'

He took a small waterproof case of wax matches from his pocket, and in a few seconds had the lantern glowing. 'Onward!' he said.

Opening the third door along the corridor revealed a short, portly man in a white shirt and dark, striped trousers and vest, tied to a large wooden chair. His exertions in trying to escape had covered his face with bands of sweat and pulled much of his shirt loose from his waistband, but his thin black tie was still properly and severely in place. 'Light!' the man said. 'Oh, bless you my friends, whoever you are.'

We worked at untying him as quickly as possible as the barge gave a series of alarming jerks and kicks under us and tilted ever more drastically. Now, in addition to its list to the starboard, there was a decided tilt aft.

'Thank you, thank you,' said the plump man as the rope came off his legs. 'They left me here to die. And for what?'

'For what, indeed?' I replied.

'It all started . . . '

'Let's wait until we're off this vessel,' Holmes interjected, 'or in a very few moments we'll be talking under water.'

We helped our rotund comrade up, although our feet were not much steadier than his, and with much slipping and sliding we made our way along the deck. An alarming shudder ran through the vessel as we reached the stern, and we quickly lowered our new friend into the rowboat and followed him down. Holmes and I manned the oars and energetically propelled ourselves away from the sinking barge, but we had gone no more than fifteen or twenty yards when the craft gave a mighty gurgle and descended beneath the water, creating a wave that pulled us back to the center of a great vortex, and then threw us up into the air like a chip of wood in a waterfall. In a trice we were drenched and our flimsy craft was waterlogged, but by some miracle we were still in the rowboat and it was still afloat. Holmes began bailing with his cap, and our guest with his right shoe, while I continued the effort to propel us away from the area.

I oriented myself by the ever-dependable North Star, and headed toward the south east. In a little while Holmes added his efforts to my own, and we were rowing across the dark waters with reasonable speed despite our craft still being half-full of water. Our plump shipmate kept bailing until he was exhausted, then spent a few minutes panting, and commenced bailing again.

It was perhaps half an hour before we spied lights in the distance indicating that the shore was somewhere ahead of us. Half an hour more and we had nosed into a beach. A small, steep, rocky beach, but nonetheless a bit of dry land, and we were grateful. The three of us climbed out of the rowboat and fell as one onto the rough sand, where we lay exhausted and immobile. I must have slept, but I have no idea of how long. When next I opened my eyes dawn had risen, and Holmes was up and doing exercises by the water's edge.

'Come, arise my friend,' he said — he must have been drunk with exercise to address me thus — 'we must make our preparations and be on our way.'

I sat up. 'Where are we off to?' I asked.

'Surely it should be obvious,' Holmes replied.

'Humor me,' I said.

'Trieste,' said Holmes. 'Wherever Wilhelm Gottsreich Sigismond von Ormstein goes, there we shall go. For whatever is happening, he is the leader or one of the leaders.'

'Is it your dislike of him that speaks?' I

asked. 'For you have often said the same of me, and seldom was it so.'

'Ah, but on occasion . . . ' Holmes said. 'But in this case it is my knowledge of the man. He would not be a member of any organization that did not let him be its leader, or at least believe that he is the leader, for he is vain and would be easily led himself.'

Our rotund friend sat up. 'Is that English which you speak?' he asked in German.

'*Ja*,' I said, switching to that language. 'It is of no importance.'

'That is what those swine that abducted me spoke when they did not want me to understand,' he said, laboriously raising himself to his knees and then to his feet. 'But they kept forgetting — and I understood much.'

'Good!' I said. 'We will all find dry clothing for ourselves, and you shall tell us all about it.'

He stood up and offered me his hand. 'I am Herr Paulus Hansel, and I thank you and your companion for saving my life.'

'On behalf of Mr. Sherlock Holmes and myself, Professor James Moriarty, I accept your thanks,' I told him, taking the offered hand and giving it a firm shake.

'I have clothing at my — oh — I don't dare go back to my hotel.' our friend's hands flew to his mouth. 'Supposing they are there waiting for me?'

'Come now,' Holmes said. 'They believe you are dead.'

'I would not disabuse them of this notion,' he said.

We walked the three or so miles back to our hotel, booked a room for Herr Hansel, and set about our ablutions and a change of clothes. We gave the concierge the task of supplying suitable garb for our rotund friend, and he treated it as though guests of the Hotel Athènes returned water soaked and bedraggled every day of the year. Perhaps they did.

It was a little after 8:00 when we met at the hotel's restaurant for breakfast. 'Now,' Holmes said, spreading orange marmalade on his croissant and turning to Herr Hansel, 'I have restrained my curiosity long enough, and you may well be possessed of information useful to us. Start with what you were doing on that barge, if you don't mind.'

Herr Hansel drained his oversized cup of hot chocolate, put the cup down with a satisfied sigh, and wiped his mustache. 'That is simple,' he said, refilling the cup from the large pitcher on the table. 'I was preparing to die. And were you gentlemen not on board, I most assuredly would have done so.'

'What caused your companions to treat you in so unfriendly a manner?' I asked.

'They were no companions of mine,' he replied. 'I am the proprietor of the Hansel and Hansel Costume Company.' he tapped himself on the chest. 'I am the second Hansel, you understand. The first Hansel, my father, retired from the business some years ago and devotes himself to apiculture.'

'Really?' asked Holmes. 'I would like to meet him.'

'Certainly,' Hansel agreed. 'I am sure he would like to thank the man who saved his son's life.'

'Yes, there is that,' Holmes agreed. 'Go

on with your story.'

'Yes. I delivered yesterday a large order of costumes to a certain Count von Kramm at the Adlerhof.'

'Hah!' Holmes interjected. We looked at him, but he merely leaned back in his chair with his arms crossed across his chest and murmured, 'continue!'

'Yes,' said Hansel. 'Well, they were naval costumes. Officers and ordinary seamen's uniforms. From shoes to caps, with insignia and ribbons and everything.'

'Fascinating,' I said. 'British Royal Navy uniforms, no doubt.'

'Why, yes,' Hansel agreed. 'And quite enough of them to have costumed the full cast of that Gilbert and Sullivan show — *Pinafore*.'

'And the name you stitched on the caps,' Holmes interjected, 'could it have been the *Royal Edgar*?'

'Indeed it was,' Hansel said, looking startled. 'How did you . . . '

'Much like this one?' Holmes asked, pulling the cap we had found out of his pocket and placing it on the table.

Hansel picked it up, examined it

carefully, crumpled the cloth in his hands and sniffed at it. 'Why, yes,' he agreed, 'this is one of ours.'

'Go on,' I said. 'How did you get yourself tied up in that cabin?'

'It was when I asked about the undergarments,' Hansel said. 'Count von Kramm seemed to take offense.'

'Undergarments?'

Hansel nodded and took a large bite of sausage. 'We were asked to supply authentic undergarments, and I went to considerable trouble to comply with his request.'

'Whatever for?' asked Holmes.

Hansel shrugged a wide, expressive shrug. 'I did not ask,' he said. 'I assumed it was for whatever production he was planning to put on. I acquired the requested undergarments from the Naval Stores at Portsmouth, so their authenticity was assured.'

'You thought it was for a play?' I asked. 'Doesn't that sound like excessive realism?'

Another shrug. 'I have heard that when Untermeyer produces a show at the

Konigliche Theater he puts loose change in the corners of the couches and stuffed chairs, and all the doors and windows on the set must open and close even if they are not to be used during the performance.'

'Who are we to question theatrical genius?' Holmes agreed. 'If Count Kramm's theatrical sailors are to wear sailors' undergarments, why then so be it.'

'Indeed,' said Hansel. 'But why only five sets?'

Holmes carefully put down his coffee cup. 'Five sets only?'

'That's right.'

'And how many sets of, ah, outer garments?'

'Thirty five complete uniforms. Twelve officers and the rest common sailors.'

'How strange,' I said.

Hansel nodded. 'That's what I said. That's why I ended up tied up on that chair, or so I suppose.'

Holmes looked at me. 'Count von Kramm,' he said, 'or as I know him better, Wilhelm Gottsreich Sigismond von Ormstein, Grand Duke of Cassel-Felstein and Hereditary King of Bohemia, dislikes being questioned.'

'I see,' I said.

'Von Kramm is one of his favorite aliases.'

'That man is a king?' Hansel asked, a note of alarm in his voice. 'There is no place where one can hide from a king.'

'Do not be alarmed,' Holmes told him. 'By now he has forgotten that you ever existed.'

'Ah, yes,' Hansel said. 'There is that about kings.'

Holmes stood. 'I think we must go to Trieste,' he said. 'There is devil's work afoot.'

'Yes,' I agreed. 'I need to send a telegram. I'll have the reply sent to Trieste.'

'I, I think, must go home,' said Hansel.

'Yes, of course,' Holmes agreed. He took Hansel's hand. 'You have earned the thanks of another royal person, and I shall see that, in the fullness of time, you are suitably rewarded.'

'You are g-going to r-r-reward me?' Hansel stammered. 'But your grace, your kingship, I had no idea. I mean . . . '

Holmes barked out a short laugh. 'No, my good man,' he said. 'Not I. A gracious lady on whose shoulders rest the weight of the greatest empire in the world.'

'Oh,' said Hansel. 'Her.'

★ ★ ★

The city of Trieste rests on the Gulf of Trieste, which is the northern tip of the Adriatic Sea, and is surrounded by mountains where it isn't fronting water. The city dates back to Roman times, and its architecture is a potpourri of every period from then to the present. Although it is putatively a part of the Austrian Empire, its citizens mostly speak Italian, and are more concerned with the happenings in Rome and Venice than those in Vienna and Budapest.

The journey took us two days by the most direct route we could find. But we reconciled ourselves with the thought that von Ormstein and his band of pseudo-English sailors couldn't have arrived much ahead of us.

During the journey we discussed what we had found out and worked out a course of action. It was necessarily vague, as although we now had a pretty good idea of what von Ormstein was planning, we didn't know what resources we would find available to us to stop him from carrying out his dastardly scheme.

Before we left Lindau, Holmes and I had sent a telegram to Mycroft:

SEND NAMES AND LOCATIONS OF ALL DESTROYERS OF ROYAL HENRY CLASS REPLY GENERAL PO TRIESTE SHERLOCK

A reply awaited us when we arrived. We retired to a nearby coffee house and perused it over steaming glasses of espresso:

EIGHT SHIPS IN CLASS ROYAL HENRY ROYAL ELIZABETH AND ROYAL ROBERT WITH ATLANTIC FLEET AT PORTSMOUTH ROYAL STEPHEN IN DRYDOCK BEING REFITTED ROYAL WILLIAM IN BAY OF BENGAL ROYAL EDWARD

AND ROYAL EDGAR ON WAY TO
AUSTRALIA ROYAL MARY DECOM-
MISSIONED SOLD TO URUGUAY
PRESUMABLY CROSSING ATLAN-
TIC TO MONTEVIDEO WHAT
NEWS MYCROFT

I slapped my hand down on the coffee
table. 'Uruguay!'

Holmes looked at me.

'Uruguay is divided into nineteen
departments,' I told him.

'That is the sort of trivia with which I
refuse to burden my mind,' he said. 'The
study of crime and criminals provides
enough intellectual . . . '

'Of which one,' I interrupted, 'is
Florida.'

He stopped, his mouth open. 'Florida?'

'Just so.'

'The letter . . . 'The Florida is now
ours.''

'It is common practice to name war-
ships after counties, states, departments,
or other subdivisions of a country,' I said.
'The British Navy has an Essex, a Sussex,
a Kent, and several others, I believe.'

Holmes thought this over. 'The conclusion is inescapable,' he said. 'The Florida . . . '

'And the undergarments,' I said.

Holmes nodded. 'When you have eliminated the impossible,' he said, 'whatever remains, however improbable, stands a good chance of being the truth.'

I shook my head. 'And you have called me the Napoleon of crime,' I said. 'Compared to this . . . '

'Ah!' said Holmes. 'But this isn't crime, this is politics. International intrigue. A much rougher game. There is no honor among politicians.'

We walked hurriedly to the British consulate on Avenue San Lucia and identified ourselves to the Consul, a white-haired, impeccably dressed statesman named Aubrey, requesting that he send a coded message to Whitehall.

He looked at us quizzically over his wire-rim glasses. 'Certainly, gentlemen,' he said. 'To what effect?'

'We are going to ask Her Majesty's government to supply us with a battleship,' Holmes said, and paused, waiting for the reaction.

It was not what one might have expected. 'There are no British battle-ships visiting the port right now,' Aubrey said, folding his hands over his ample stomach and leaning back in his chair. 'Will a cruiser do?'

Holmes leaned over the desk. 'We are in earnest,' he said, his intense eyes glowering over his thin, ascetic nose, 'and this is not a jest. To the contrary, it is of the utmost importance and urgency.'

'I have no doubt,' replied Aubrey, looking up mildly. 'My offer was sincere. If a cruiser will suffice, I am ready to put one at your disposal. It's all that's available. There are some four or five Royal Navy torpedo gunboats working with the Italian Navy engaged in the suppression of smugglers and pirates in the Mediterranean, but I can't predict when one of them will come to port.'

'But you're prepared to put a cruiser at, er, our disposal?' I asked.

'I am,' said Aubrey, nodding. 'That is, I have no direct authority to do so, but the authority has been passed on to me from

Whitehall. I received a cable this morning directing me to do all I could to assist you, were you to show up. I must say I've never been given an instruction like that before in eighteen years in the Foreign Service. From the P.M. himself, don't you know. Along with a screed from the Admiralty.'

Holmes straightened up. 'Mycroft!' he said.

'Undoubtedly,' I agreed.

'Her Majesty's Ship *Agamemnon* is in port,' said Aubrey, 'and I have passed on the request of the Admiralty to Captain Preisner that he keep steam up and to await further instructions. Now, if you could tell me what this is all about, perhaps I could be of some further assistance.'

'Let us head to the docks immediately,' Holmes said. 'We will explain on the way.'

Aubrey reached for the bell pull behind his desk. 'Call up my carriage,' he told the man who appeared in answer to his summons. 'And fetch my greatcoat, there's a chill in the air.'

Consul Aubrey gave instructions, and

soon we were racing through the streets of Trieste heading toward the municipal docks, where a waiting launch would take us to the *Agamemnon*. 'In case something goes wrong,' Holmes told the Consul, 'and there's every chance it will, you'll have to prepare.'

'Prepare for what?' Aubrey asked. 'In what way?'

Holmes and I took it in turns to tell him what we knew and what we surmised. 'We may not have all the details correct,' I said, 'but if events do not unfold much as we have described, I will be greatly surprised.'

'But this is incredible!' Aubrey said. 'How did you figure all this out?'

'No time now,' Holmes declared as the carriage pulled to a stop. 'We must hurry.'

'Good luck,' Aubrey said. 'I shall return to the consulate and prepare for your success or failure, whichever comes from this madness.'

'It must sound mad,' I agreed. 'But it is not our madness, but that of our antagonist.'

'Come,' said Holmes. 'Let us board the launch.'

We leapt aboard the steam launch. The boatswain saluted us as we raced past him down the gangway and then blew on his whistle twice, and we were off. The harbor was thick with shipping, and we weaved and dodged between vessels of all sorts and sizes, making our way to the great, looming bulk of the three-stack cruiser of modern design that was our destination.

When we reached the *Agamemnon* a ladder was lowered from the deck of the cruiser to receive us. The sea was calm in the harbor, but transferring from the rolling deck of the steam launch to the pitching ladder at the cruiser's side, even in those gentle swells, was more of an effort than a sedate unadventuresome man of my years found enjoyable.

Captain Preisner's flag officer met us as we stepped onto the deck, and led he way to the bridge of the *Agammenon*, where Preisner, a thin man with a bony face and a short, pointed gray beard, greeted us warily. 'Mr. Holmes, he said, with a stiff nod of his head, 'Professor Moriarty. Welcome, I think, to the *Agamemnon.*'

'Captain,' I acknowledged.

Preisner flapped a sheet of yellow paper at us. 'I am requested and required by the Admiralty to give you whatever assistance you require, without asking questions. Or, at least, without demanding answers. Which, I must say are the oddest instructions I have ever received.'

'This may be the oddest mission you will ever engage in,' Holmes told him.

Captain Preisner sighed. 'And somehow I have the feeling that it will not bring accolades to me or my crew,' he said.

'You will probably be requested not to mention it in your official report,' I told him. 'And, were I you, I would not enter the details in my log until I had time to think deeply on it.'

'It was ever thus,' Preisner said. 'What am I to do?'

I pointed to the south. 'Somewhere out there, not too far away, is a destroyer flying the Union Jack, or possibly the Red

Ensign. We have to stop it and board it. Or, if that proves impossible, sink it.'

Preisner looked at me, speechless. And then he looked at Holmes, who nodded. 'Sink a British warship?' he asked incredulously.

'Ah,' Holmes said, 'but it isn't. And if we do not succeed in stopping it, some major outrage will be committed in the harbor of Trieste or some nearby coastal city, and it will be blamed on the British Navy.'

'A ruse of war?' Preisner asked. 'But we aren't at war, that I know of.'

'We'd better consider it a 'ruse of peace,' then,' Holmes said. 'Although the ultimate purpose of the exercise might well be to provoke a state of war between Britain and several continental powers.'

'A Royal Navy destroyer,' Preisner mused, 'that *isn't* a Royal Navy destroyer.'

'The name on her side will be *Royal Edgar*, I told him. 'In reality she is the decommissioned *Royal Mary*, which has been sold to Uruguay. The Uruguayan government, we believe, renamed her the *Florida*.'

'We're going to war with Uruguay?'

'She is now in the hands of a group of rogue European, ah, gentlemen, who plan to use her to provoke animosity and, perhaps, active hostilities against Great Britain. How the transfer was made from the Uruguayan authorities to the plotters remains to be seen. It could well be that the government of Uruguay knows nothing of the supposed sale.'

'My god! How did you — never mind that now!' Preisner swung around and barked out a series of orders, which got the great ship underway.

While the *Agamemnon* made her way out into the Gulf of Trieste and headed down the Adriatic Sea, Captain Preisner concerned himself with the handling of his ship, but once we were in open water he turned the helm over to Lieutenant Willits, his bulldog-jawed, taciturn first officer, and called us to his side. 'Now tell me what you know,' he said, 'and what you surmise, so that we can plan a course of action.'

As rapidly as possible, but leaving out nothing of consequence, we told him our story. Holmes took the lead, and in that nasal, high-pitched voice of his outlined what we knew and how we had learned it.

Preisner rested his elbows on the ledge running around the front of the bridge, directly below the large glass windscreens, and stared out at the choppy blue-green sea. 'And on these meager facts you have commandeered one of Her Majesty's battle cruisers and set out in search of a destroyer that may or may not exist, and that, if it does exist, may or may not be planning some harm to British interests? And the Lords of the Admiralty have agreed with this, ah, unlikely interpretation?' he shook his head. 'I will obey orders, even if it means obeying *your* orders and racing up and down the Adriatic, but frankly I don't see it.'

'You don't agree that it is likely that this cabal has gotten possession of the *Royal Mary* and intends harm to Britain?' Holmes asked.

Of what possible profit to them could such an action be?' Preisner asked. 'I grant you your conclusion that these people were training a crew to operate a

British warship, and the *Royal Mary* might well be the one. And if they were planning to come to Trieste, then they were probably picking up the ship somewhere around here. But is it not more likely that, having obtained the ship, they will take it to some distant port to commit their outrage, if indeed an outrage is planned?'

'There are several reasons to believe that, whatever sort of attack they are planning, it will be nearby and soon,' I said.

'For one thing,' said Holmes, 'their men cannot be all that well trained in the handling of a modern destroyer.'

'For another,' I added, 'every extra hour they spend will increase the likelihood that they will be intercepted by some ship of Her Majesty's Mediterranean Fleet. And one attempt to exchange signals would brand her as an imposter.'

'For maximum effect,' Holmes said, 'the outrage should be conducted close to a city or large town, so that it will be observed by as many people as possible.'

'That makes sense,' Preisner agreed.

'And then there are the undergarments,' I said.

'Yes,' Holmes agreed. 'That gives the whole game away.'

'Captain Preisner looked from one to the other of us. 'It does?' he asked.

A mess steward came by with steaming mugs of tea for those on bridge, and he had thoughtfully included two for Holmes and me.

I took the tea gratefully and sipped at it. Neither Holmes nor I were dressed for the chill breeze that whipped through the open doors of the bridge. 'The men in the Royal Navy uniforms are to be visible on deck during the event,' I told Captain Preisner, 'so that watchers on shore will believe the masquerade. But why undergarments?'

'And why only five?' Holmes added.

Preisner looked thoughtful. 'A good question,' he said.

'The only reasonable answer is that those five men must pass close inspection when their bodies are examined.'

'Their bodies?'

'Consider,' said Holmes. 'The under-garments only make sense if it is expected that the men will be examined.'

'Yes, I see that,' Preisner agreed.

'But if they are alive when they are examined, any discrepancies will become quickly evident,' said Holmes.

'As, for instance, their not speaking fluent English,' I added.

'So you think they are dressing corpses in British naval uniforms?' Preisner asked.

Holmes looked away. 'Perhaps,' he said.

'Sail ho to the port!' a seaman outside the bridge relayed a call from the lookout on the top mast. We turned to look, but it was indeed a sail, the topsail of a three-masted barque, and not the four funnels of a British destroyer, that slowly came into sight on our port side.

We saw a variety of ships during the rest of that day, but it was dusk before we found the ship we were seeking. A four-masted destroyer appeared in the distance a few points off the starboard bow. Lieutenant Willits grabbed for the chart of identification silhouettes and ran his finger down the side while peering closely at the illustrations. 'I don't believe there would be any other four-masted destroyer in the area,' he said, 'but it would not do to make a mistake.'

Captain Preisner examined the distant ship through his binoculars and, even before Willits had confirmed the identification, turned to the duty seaman and said quietly, 'Signal all hands — battle stations.'

The seaman whistled down the communications tube and relayed the command and, almost immediately, an ordered bedlam descended on the boat as the members of the crew raced to their assigned positions.

'She's flying no flags or pennants,' announced Willits, who was staring at the approaching ship through his own binoculars. 'But she's making no attempt to avoid us. There appears to be a small black ship of some sort to her rear.'

'It would look suspicious were she to turn aside,' said Preisner. 'She doesn't know that we're stalking her. Hoist our own flag and the recognition code flag for today. And see if you can identify the ship to her rear.'

'Aye, aye, sir.' Willits relayed the command, and in a few seconds several flags were fluttering at the top of the *Agamemnon's* forward mast.

'No response,' said Willits after a minute. 'Wait — she's turning to port, trying to evade us. If she complete's the turn, she'll be able to show us her heels. She must have three or four knots better speed.'

'Probably less with an untrained engine crew,' commented Preisner. 'But nonetheless — '

'I can make out her name now,' said Willits, peering through his binoculars. 'She's the *Royal Edgar*, right enough. Or claims she is. The other ship is keeping on her far side, but it appears to be some sort of large yacht, painted black.'

'A smuggler, no doubt,' said Preisner.

'I believe you're right, sir.'

'Put a warning shot across her bow and run up the signal for 'Come to a complete stop',' directed the captain. 'Helmsman, turn twenty degrees to the starboard.'

One of the *Agamemnon's* four-inch guns barked once, and a fountain of water

186

appeared off the bow of the *Royal Edgar*.

The destroyer continuing turning, ignoring the warning. The *Agamemnon* fired another shot, which plunged into the water close enough to have soaked anyone standing by the bow of the *Royal Edgar*. A few seconds later one of the *Royal Edgar*'s two-inch guns coughed a burst of flame, and an explosion sounded somewhere forward on the cruiser. A few seconds later, another burst, and a sound like the banging together of a hundred large iron pots came from amidships.

'They're firing at us!' yelled Lieutenant Willits.

'More fools they,' said Captain Preisner grimly, and he gave the order to return fire.

The universe became filled with awesome roaring sounds as the eight-inch guns of the *Agamemnon* hurled their hundred and twenty pound explosive missiles into the air. In two minutes the firing from the *Royal Edgar* had stopped, and Captain Preisner gave the order for our own ship to cease fire. A total of no more than a dozen rounds had been fired by the big guns of the cruiser, but the damage done to the destroyer gave one faith in the might of modern science. She was dead in the water and already starting to list to one side. Billows of smoke were coming from amidships, and a tongue of flame was growing toward the bow.

The black yacht had pulled up alongside the *Royal Edgar* now, and people were transferring over. Others were attempting to lower a lifeboat aft of the bridge.

'We should board her, Captain,' Holmes said.

'Why?' asked Preisner.

'There may be documents.'

'There may be wounded,' added Lieutenant Willits.

'I'll have a boat lowered and ask for volunteers to row you over,' Preisner told us. 'But I'm not bringing the *Agamemnon* anywhere near that vessel. And I warn you, she's either going to blow up or go under quite soon, and quite suddenly.'

Volunteers were found — the human race never ceases to astound me — and the captain's gig was lowered. We armed ourselves with revolvers and knives from a locker on the bridge, and we were shortly being rowed over to the *Royal Edgar*, which was not any lower in the water, although the fire was still burning. As we approached, the black yacht roared past us headed off toward the south. A portly man in a Royal Navy officer's uniform standing rigidly in the rear of the yacht shook his fist at us as he passed.

'Would that be the king?' I asked Holmes.

'I believe it is,' Holmes told me. 'Yes, I believe it is.'

We instructed our oarsmen to remain in the gig and to row rapidly away at the first sign that something untoward was about to happen.

'But what about yourselves, governor?' asked the bo's'n in charge of the rowing party.

'We shall dive off the ship and swim rapidly toward the *Agamemnon*,' I told him.

'We'll probably be there before you are,' Holmes added.

'Very good, sir,' responded the bo's'n,

but he was not convinced.

A couple of ropes were visible dangling over the side of the destroyer, and I grabbed one of them and pulled myself up. Holmes waited until I was on deck to follow me up the rope. There was very little damage evident on deck. Were it not for the smoke behind us and the fire ahead of us, it would look like there was nothing amiss.

'Why do you suppose they fled,' Holmes asked, 'instead of attempting to fight the fire?'

'Perhaps they were not trained to do so,' I responded. 'Perhaps they didn't have the equipment.'

'Perhaps,' Holmes agreed.

We had boarded amidships. By some unspoken agreement, we both turned and went forward. 'If there are any useful documents,' I said, 'they're probably in the bridge.'

'If there were any,' Holmes replied, 'Wilhelm Gottsreich most assuredly took them with him.'

'Perhaps,' I said.

We reached the ladder leading up to

the bridge, and Holmes went up ahead of me. He stopped, frozen, in the doorway, and I could not get by. 'What is it, Holmes,' I asked, trying to peer around his shoulder.

'As I feared,' he said, 'but could not bring myself to believe . . . ' He moved into the room, and I entered behind him.

There, lined up against the back wall, were four men in the uniforms of ordinary seamen in the Royal Navy. Their hands and feet were tied, and their mouths were covered with sticking plaster. One of them seemed to have fainted; he was slumped over, only held up by the rope around his chest which was affixed to a metal hook in the wall. The other three were conscious: one trembling uncontrollably, one rigidly staring out the windscreen, his face frozen with shock, and the third fighting like a trapped beast against his bonds; his wrists raw, and blood streaming from his forehead.

A fifth man, his hands still tied behind him, lay prone on the floor, his face immersed in a large pan of water. He did not move. Holmes ran over to him, pulled up his head and rolled him over. After a few seconds he got up from the still body. 'Too late,' he said.

We used our knives to free the other men and, grabbing what papers we could find without bothering to look through them, led the men back down the ladder and out to the gig. Twenty minutes later we were aboard the *Agamemnon*, and the *Royal Edgar* was still burning, but was no lower in the water and her list seemed not to have increased.

'We can't leave her like this,' Captain Preisner said, 'and I can't tow her in; too many questions would be asked.'

'You'll have to sink her,' Holmes said.

Captain Preisner nodded. 'Order the main batteries to fire ten rounds each, controlled fire, at the destroyer,' he told the bridge duty officer.

About ten minutes after the last round was fired the destroyer gave a tremendous belch, and sunk prow first into the sea. The entire crew of the *Agamemnon*, having been informed that it was a sister ship they were forced to sink, stood silently at attention as she went down. Captain Preisner held a salute until the one-time Royal Mary was out of sight beneath the waves, as did all the officers on the bridge.

Captain Preisner sighed and relaxed. 'I hope I never have to do anything like that again,' he said.

Later that evening Captain Preisner called us into his cabin. 'I have a berth for you,' he said. 'We won't be back in port again until late tomorrow.'

'That's fine, Captain,' I said. 'We still have to compose our report to send back to Whitehall.'

Preisner looked at us. 'Those men you brought aboard — you spoke to them?'

'We did.'

'And?'

'The five suits of undergarments,' Holmes said.

'But you only brought four men along.'

'True,' Holmes said. 'Our antagonist had begun preparing for his assault. One of the men was already drowned. The others would have joined him shortly had we not come upon the ship when we did.

The plan was to chase the black yacht in to the Trieste harbor, getting as close to the city as possible. Then fire some shots at the fleeing craft, which would miss and hit at random in the city. Then the destroyer would, itself, flee back out to sea. A small explosion, presumably caused by the yacht firing back, would cause the five drowned men to be flung into the water, there to be found in their Royal Navy uniforms by the locals.'

Captain Preisner stared at him speechless for a long moment. 'And all this,' he said finally, 'to discredit England?' he asked. 'What good would it do?'

'Major conflagrations are started by small sparks,' Holmes said. 'Who can say where this might have led?'

Preisner shook his head. 'Madmen,' he said.

'Even so,' Holmes agreed. 'There are an abundance of them.'

Later in our cabin Holmes turned to me and asked, 'what are you planning to do after we send our report?'

I shrugged. 'The world thinks I am dead,' I said. 'Perhaps I shall take advantage of that and remain away from public ken.'

'I, also, had thought of doing something of the sort,' Holmes told me. 'I've always wanted to travel to Tibet, perhaps speak with the Dali Lama.'

'A very interesting man,' I told him. 'I'm sure you'd find such a conversation fruitful.'

Holmes stared at me for a long time, and then said 'Good night, Professor,' and turned down the light.

'Good night, Holmes,' I replied.

3

The Paradol Paradox

It is a damp, chilly Saturday, the 16th of April, 1887, as I sit before the small coal fire in the front room of Professor James Moriarty's Russell Square home making these notes; setting down while they are still fresh in my memory the queer and astounding events surrounding the problem with which professor Moriarty and I found ourselves involved over the past few days. The case itself, a matter of some delicacy involving some of the highest-born and most important personages in the realm, had, as Moriarty put it, 'a few points that were not entirely devoid of interest to the higher faculties.' Moriarty's ability to shed light on what the rest of us find dark and mysterious will come as no surprise to anyone who has had any dealings with the professor. But what will keep the events of these past days unique in my mind forever is the glimpse I was afforded into the private life of my friend and mentor, Professor James Moriarty.

Certain aspects of the case will never see print, at least not during the lifetimes of any of those involved; and I certainly cannot write it up in one of my articles for the American press, without revealing what must not be revealed. But the facts should not be lost, so I will at least set them down here, and if this notebook remains locked in the bottom drawer of my desk at my office at the American News Service until after my death, so be it. At least the future will learn what must be concealed from the present.

My name is Benjamin Barnett, and I am an expatriate New Yorker, working here in London as the director and owner of the American News Service; a company that sends news and feature stories from Britain and the continent to newspapers all around the United States over the Atlantic cable. Four years ago I was rescued from an unfortunate circumstance — and being held prisoner in a Turkish fortress is as unfortunate a circumstance as I can imagine that does not involve immediate great pain or disfigurement — by Professor James Moriarty. I was employed by him for two years after that, and found him to be one of the most intelligent, perceptive, capable; in short one of the wisest men I have ever known. Most of those who have had dealings with the professor would, I am sure, agree, with the notable exception of a certain consulting detective, who places Moriarty at the center of every nefarious plot hatched by anyone, anywhere, during this past quarter-century. I have no idea why he persists in this invidious belief. I have seen that the professor sometimes skirts the law to achieve his own ends, but I can also witness that Professor Moriarty has a higher moral standard than many of those who enforce it.

But I digress. It was last Tuesday evening, four days ago, that saw the start of the events I relate. We had just finished dinner and I was still sitting at the dining table, drinking my coffee and reading a back issue of *The Strand Magazine*.

Moriarty was staring moodily out the window, his long, aristocratic fingers twitching with boredom. He was waiting, at the time, for a new spectrograph of his own design to be completed so that he could continue his researches into the spectral lines of one of the nearer stars. When he is not engaged in his scientific endeavors, Moriarty likes to solve problems of a more earthly nature, but at the moment there was no such exercise to engage his intellect; and to Professor Moriarty intellect was all.

I finished the article I was reading, closed the magazine, and shook my head in annoyance.

'You're right,' Moriarty said without turning from the window. 'It is shameful the way the Austrian medical establishment treated Dr. Semmelweis. Pass me a cigar, would you, old chap?'

'Not merely the Austrians,' I said, putting the magazine down and reaching for the humidor on the mantle. 'The whole medical world. But really, Moriarty, this is too much. Two hundred years ago they would have burned you at the stake as a sorcerer.'

Moriarty leaned over and took a cigar from the humidor as I held it toward him. 'After all the time we have been in association,' he said, 'surely you can follow my methods by now.'

'It is one thing to watch from the audience as De Kolta vanishes a girl on stage,' I told him, 'quite another to know how the trick is done.'

Moriarty smiled and rolled the cigar between his palms. 'My 'tricks' are in one way quite like those of a stage conjurer,' he said. 'Once you know how they're done, they don't seem quite so miraculous.' He paused to clip and pierce the ends of the cigar with his silver cigar cutter. Then he lit a taper from the gas mantle on the wall, and puffed the cigar to life. 'But think back. This particular miracle should succumb even to your analysis.'

I rose and went over to the sideboard to pour myself another cup of coffee. The serving girl had yet to clear away the dinner dishes, and I absently banged the coffee spoon against a wine glass that had recently held its share of a fine '63 *Chateau de Braquenne* Bordeaux. Some months ago Moriarty had cleared up a particularly delicate problem for Hamish Plummet, partner in Plummet & Rose, Wines and Spirits, Piccadilly. Plummet presented the professor with a case of that rare vintage as a token of his appreciation, and tonight Moriarty had uncorked a bottle and pronounced it excellent. I was pleased to agree.

'You read the article,' I suggested.

'Bravo, Barnett,' Moriarty said. 'A capital start.'

'And you saw me reading it. But wait — you were across the room, looking out the window.'

'True,' Moriarty acknowledged. 'I saw you reflected in the window glass.'

'Ah!' I said. 'But how did you know which article — even if you saw me reading — '

'I did not merely see, I observed. You stared down at your free hand, turning it over and examining it in a contemplative manner.'

'Did I?'

'You were reflecting on Semmelweis's campaign to get his fellow physicians to wash their hands before treating patients. You were no doubt thinking of how many poor women had died in childbirth because the doctors scorned him and refused to take his advice.'

'That's so, I remember,' I told him.

'Thus I knew, by observation, which article you were reading. And then you put down the magazine and shook your head, clearly revealing your sequence of thought, and I said what I said.' Moriarty returned his gaze to the window and puffed silently on his cigar.

A few moments later Mr. Maws, Moriarty's butler, knocked at the door and entered, and the serving girl scurried in past him and started clearing the table. 'There's a milord come to see you, Professor,' he said. 'I put him in the front room. Here's his lordship's card.' Mr. Maws handed Moriarty the rectangular pasteboard.

Moriarty centered his cigar carefully on the lip of an oversized ashtray and looked at the card, and then looked again. He ran his fingers over the surface, and then reached for a glass of water on the table, using it as a magnifying glass to carefully study the printing on the card. 'Fascinating,' he said. 'What does the milord look like?'

'Young,' Mr. Maws pronounced. 'His attire is a bit on the messy side.'

'Ah!' Moriarty said. 'Well, I'll see him in my office. Give us a few seconds to get settled, and then bring him along.'

'Very good, Professor,' Mr. Maws said, and he bowed slightly and backed out of the room.

'The nobility has a sobering effect on Mr. Maws,' Moriarty commented, as we crossed the hall to the office.

'Who is it, Professor?' I asked. 'A client?'

Moriarty passed me the card. 'Certainly he desires to become one,' he said. 'Else why would he come calling at this time of night?'

I examined the card to see what had fascinated Moriarty. Printed on the face was: *Lord Everett Tams*, and underneath that: *Earl of Whitton.* There was nothing else. 'Then you don't know who he is?'

'No.' Moriarty went to the bookshelf by his desk and reached for the copy of *Burke's Peerage*, then took his hand away. 'And we don't have time to look him up, either, if those are his footsteps I hear.'

I sat down on a chair by the window and awaited events.

A few seconds later a harried-looking man of thirty-five or so in a rumpled dark suit burst through the door and stared at both our faces before deciding which of us he had come to see. 'Professor Moriarty,' he said, addressing my companion, who had lowered himself into the massive leather chair behind his desk, 'I am in the deepest trouble. You must help me!'

'Of course, your lordship. Sit down, compose yourself, and tell me your problem. I think you will find this chair by the desk comfortable.'

His lordship dropped into the chair and looked from one to the other of us, his hands clasped tightly in front of him.

'This is Mr. Barnett, my companion

and confidant,' Moriarty told the distraught lord. Anything you choose to tell me will be safe with him.'

'Yes, of course,' Lord Tams said. 'It's not that. Only — I'm not sure how to begin.'

'Let me see if I can help,' Moriarty said, leaning forward and resting his chin on his tented hands. His hawk-like eyes looked Lord Tams over closely for a few seconds. 'You are unmarried. Your older brother died unexpectedly quite recently, leaving you heir to the title and, presumably, estates of the Earldom of Whitton. Your new obligations make it necessary for you to give up your chosen profession of journalism, a result that is not altogether pleasing to you. You and your brother were not on the best of terms, although nothing irreconcilable had passed between you.'

His lordship's hands dropped to his side and he stared at Moriarty. The professor has that effect on some people.

Moriarty sat up. 'There are some other indications that are suggestive but not certain,' he said. 'As to the specific problem that brought you here, I'm afraid you'll have to tell me what it is.'

'Who has spoken to you about me?' Lord Tams demanded.

'No one, your lordship, I assure you,' Moriarty said. 'You carry the indications about for the trained eye to read.'

'Really?' Lord Tams rested one hand firmly on the edge of the desk and pointed an accusing finger at Moriarty with the other. 'The death of my brother? The fact that I am unmarried — and a journalist? Come now, sir!'

Moriarty leaned forward, his eyes bright. 'It is, after all, my profession, my lord,' he said. 'My ability to see what others cannot is, presumably, what brought you to me. Now, what is your problem?'

Lord Tams took a deep breath, or perhaps it was a sigh. 'Your surmises are correct, Professor Moriarty,' he said. 'I am unmarried. My profession, if such I may call it, has been writing freelance articles on economic subjects for various London newspapers and magazines. When an editor wants a piece on free trade, or Servian war reparations, he calls on me. I have recently — very recently — come into the title, inheriting it from my elder brother Vincent, who died suddenly. It is his death that has brought me here to seek your assistance.'

I leaned forward in my chair. The thrill of being in at the beginning of one of Moriarty's little exercises does not diminish with time. 'Your brother was murdered?' I asked.

'My brother's death was, and is, completely unexplainable, Mr. Barnett,' Lord Tams replied.

Moriarty clapped his hands together. 'Really?' he said. 'Come, this is quite — interesting. Tell me everything you know of the affair.'

'The circumstances are simple. Vincent had gone to one of his clubs — the Paradol in Montague Street — to stay for a few days. On the morning of the third day a waiter went in to bring Vincent his breakfast, which he had ordered the night before, and found my brother dead in his bed. He was lying on his back, his face and chest unnaturally red, his hands were raised as if to ward off some unseen threat, and a look of terror was fixed on his face. The club doctor, a Dr. Papoli, examined him and said it was apoplexy; but, as the doctor is from somewhere in the Balkans, and lacks a British medical degree, nobody seemed to take him too seriously. The police doctor strongly disagreed, although he could not come up with an alternate diagnosis.'

'This was at the Paradol, you say? Did your brother commonly frequent the Paradol Club?'

'He has been a member for years,' his lordship said, 'going perhaps six or seven times a year. But for the past three months he had been going twice a month, and staying for two or three days each time.'

'Are you also a member?'

'I am a permanent guest of my brother's,' his lordship said. 'I occasionally use the reading room, but as for the club's other — functions — I found that they were not to my taste.'

'I don't believe I know the club,' I said to Moriarty.

'It is for, ah, specialized interests,' Moriarty told me. 'It is where rich men go to meet with complaisant women. It is an upper-class rendezvous for what the French call *le demi-monde*. The French seem to have a word for everything, have you noticed?'

'It is so,' Lord Tams agreed. 'The Paradol Club exists for those gentlemen who enjoy the company of women of, let us say, loose morals but impeccable manners. It is not the only establishment of its type in London, but it is one of the most exclusive, expensive, and discreet.'

'Did your brother express his taste for these sorts of amusements in any other way?' Moriarty asked.

'His whole life revolved around the pleasures of the senses. It's funny, really; Mama was always pleased that Vincent didn't go in for blood sports. She never guessed the sort of sport in which he did indulge.'

Moriarty leaned back in his chair and fixed his gaze on Lord Tams. 'When was the last time you saw your brother?' he asked.

'The evening before he died.'

'Ah! Under what circumstances?'

'I went to see him at the club to ask a favor of him. I am — I was — getting married. I wanted to advance some money from my allowance.'

'Allowance?' Moriarty asked. 'Then you had nothing on your own?'

'Upon our father's death the entire estate went to Vincent. The house and lands were, of course, entailed, but Vincent also inherited everything else. It was inadvertent. Vincent was fourteen years older than I, and the will was drawn two years before I was born. My parents did not expect another child, and no provision was made in the will for the unexpected. My father died suddenly shortly before my second birthday, and had not gotten around to revising the will.'

'I see,' Moriarty said.

'My brother has actually been quite generous,' Lord Tams said. 'The income of a freelance journalist is precarious at best. Vincent gave me an allowance and added a few odd bob here and there when needed.'

'How did you feel about his — indulgences?'

'It was not my place to approve or disapprove. Vincent's penchants were his own business. His habits, as he kept reminding me, hurt no one. His view was that his companions were all willing, and profited from the relationship. I remonstrated with him, pointing out that the path of vice spirals ever downward, and that the further along it one travels, the harder it is to get off.'

'He didn't listen?'

'He was amused.'

'Yes. And you went to see him because you're getting married?'

'I have been engaged to Miss Margot Whitsome, the poetess, for the past two years. We were to have been married next week.'

'Were to have been? Then the ceremony has been called off?'

'Delayed, rather.'

'By the poetess?'

'By me. How can I allow any lady of breeding to marry me with this hanging over my head?'

'Ah!' Moriarty said. 'You are suspected of murdering your brother?'

Our newly-ennobled visitor stood and walked to the window, staring out into the dark evening drizzle. 'No one has said anything directly,' he said. 'But I have been questioned by Scotland Yard twice, each time a bit more sharply. My fellow journalists are beginning to regard me as a potential story rather than a colleague. An inspector named Lestrade has been up to see my editor at the *Evening Standard* to ask if I've ever written anything on tropical poisons.'

'How imaginative of him,' Moriarty commented.

Our visitor turned sharply. 'Professor Moriarty, I have been told that you can solve the unsolvable; that you can see clearly where others find only darkness. I hope this is true, for otherwise I see nothing but darkness ahead of me,' he said. 'I want you to find out what happened to my brother. If he was murdered, I want you to find out who did it. If he met his death by some natural means, I want you to discover the agency that brought it about. My peace of mind and my future happiness depend upon your success! You can name your fee!'

Moriarty rose and took Lord Tams' hand. 'First let me solve your little problem,' he said, 'then we'll discuss the price.'

After some further reassurances, Moriarty sent Lord Tams back out into Russell Square, assuring him that he would have some word for him soon.

'All right,' Moriarty,' I said when we were again alone. 'By what feat of legerdemain did you deduce all that? Did you pick the man's pocket as he entered the room?'

'Deduce what?' Moriarty asked, settling back down in his chair. 'Oh, you mean — '

'Yes, I mean,' I agreed.

'Nothing extraordinary,' Moriarty said. 'That he was unmarried I deduced from the state of his clothing. No respectable woman would let her husband go out with his suit unpressed and a tear in the jacket pocket. That also told me that he does not yet employ the services of a valet. That his older brother died quite recently I deduced from his calling card. The lower line of type was of a slightly different font than the upper, also the spacing between the two lines was slightly off. The second line was added, probably by one of those small hand presses that you find around printer's offices. The missing valet and the calling card surely indicate that he became the Earl of Whitton quite recently. And he hasn't come into the estate quite yet, or he surely would have had new cards printed, and probably bought a new suit. The hand press also pointed me in the direction of his profession. The column proof that was stuffed into his right-hand jacket pocket completed that deduction.'

'His suit looked fine to me,' I commented.

'Yes, it would,' Moriarty said. 'Anything else?'

'How did you know it was an older brother who died? Why not his father?'

'If it were his father, then he would have expected to inherit at some time, and the conflict between career and

214

station would have been resolved long since. No, it was clearly the unexpected death of an older brother that has created this dilemma for him.'

'And the antipathy between him and his brother?'

'A glance at his right sleeve showed me the pinholes where a black armband had been. The band had not been tacked on, and the pinholes had not enlarged with wear. His period of mourning for his brother was brief. Surely that suggests a certain coolness between them?'

'But not irreconcilable?'

'Certainly not. After all, he did wear the armband.'

'Ah!' I said.

The next morning Moriarty disappeared before breakfast and returned just as I was finishing my coffee. 'I have been to Scotland Yard,' he said, drawing off his coat and hanging it on a peg by the door. 'This exercise is promising indeed. I have sent the mummer out to procure copies of the last two months' *London Daily Gazette*. The crime news is more complete, if a bit more lurid, in the

Gazette. Is there more coffee?'

'What did you learn at Scotland Yard?' I asked, pouring him a cup.

'The inquest has been postponed at the request of the medical office, who are still trying to determine the cause of death. The defunct earl may have suffered from apoplexy, as diagnosed by Dr. Papoli, probably on the basis of the red face, but that did not cause his death. There are indications of asphyxiation, but nothing that could have caused it, and two deep puncture marks on his neck. The two pathologists who have been consulted can agree on nothing except their disagreement with Dr. Papoli's findings.'

I put down my coffee cup. 'Puncture marks — my dear Moriarty!'

Moriarty sipped his coffee. 'No, Barnett,' he said. 'They are not the marks of a vampire, and neither are they the punctures of a viper. They are too wide apart, coming low on the neck and almost under the ear on each side of his head. There are some older puncture marks also, in odd places; on the inner thighs and under the arms. They do not seem to have contributed to his death, but what purpose they served is unknown.'

Moriarty drank a second cup of coffee, staring at the fireplace, apparently deep in thought. Then Mummer Tolliver, Moriarty's midget-of-all-work, came in with bundles of newspapers, and Moriarty began slowly going through them. 'It is as I remembered,' he said finally. 'Look here, Barnett: the naked body of a young man was found floating in the Thames last week, with two unexplained puncture marks.'

'In his neck?' I asked.

'In his upper arms. And here — three weeks previously the body of a girl, clad only in her shift, was discovered in a field in Lower Norwood. She had what the Gazette describes as 'strange bruises' on her legs.'

'Is that significant?' I asked.

'Scotland Yard doesn't think so,' Moriarty said. After a moment's reflection he put down the paper and jumped to his feet. 'Come, Barnett!' he cried.

'Where?' I asked, struggling into my jacket.

'Since we cannot get satisfactory answers as to the manner of Lord Vincent Tams' death, we must inquire into the manner of his life. We are going to Abelard Court.'

'I thought the Paradol Club was in Montague Street.'

'It is,' Moriarty said, clapping his hat on his head and taking up his stick. 'But we go to Abelard Court. Come along!'

We waved down a passing hansom cab, Moriarty shouted an address to the driver, and we were off. 'I must tell you, Barnett,' Moriarty said, turning to face me in the cab. 'We are going to visit a lady who is a good friend and is very important to me. Society would forbid us calling her a 'lady,' but society is a fool.'

'Important to you how?' I asked.

Moriarty stared at me for a moment. 'We have shared events in our lives that have drawn us very close,' he said. 'I trust her as fully as I trust myself.'

The address the hansom cab let us off in front of was a paradigm of middle-class virtue, as was the lady's maid who answered the door, though her costume was a bit too French for the more conservative household.

'Is Mrs. Atterleigh at home?' Moriarty asked. 'Would you tell her that Professor Moriarty and a friend are calling?'

The maid curtseyed and showed us to a drawing room that was decorated in pink and light blue, and filled with delicate, finely-detailed furniture that bespoke femininity. Any male would feel rough and clumsy and out of place in this room.

After a brief wait, Mrs. Atterleigh entered the drawing room. One of those ageless mortals who, in form and gesture, encompass the mystery that is woman, she might have been nineteen, or forty, I cannot say. And no man would care. Her long brown hair framed a perfect oval face and intelligent brown eyes. She wore a red silk housedress that I cannot describe, not being adept at such things, but I could not but note that it showed more of her than I had ever seen of a woman to whom I was not married. I did not find it offensive.

'Professor!' she said, holding out her arms.

Moriarty stepped forward. 'Beatrice!'

She kissed him firmly on the cheek and released him. 'It has been too long,' she said.

'I have a favor to ask,' Moriarty said.

'I, who owe you everything, can refuse you nothing,' she replied.

Moriarty turned. 'This is my friend and colleague, Mr. Barnett,' he said.

Beatrice took my hand and firmly shook it. 'Any friend of Professor Moriarty has a call on my affections,' she said. 'And a man whom Professor Moriarty calls 'colleague' must be worthy indeed.'

'Ahem,' I said.

She released my hand and turned to again clasp both of Moriarty's hands in hers. 'Professor Moriarty rescued me from a man who, under the guise of benevolence, was the incarnation of evil.'

I resisted the impulse to pull out my notebook then and there. 'Who?' I asked.

'The monster who was my husband, Mr. Gerald Atterleigh,' she replied.

'Moriarty, you never — ' I began.

'It was before you joined my organization,' Moriarty said. 'And I didn't discuss it later because there were aspects of the events that are better forgotten.'

'Thanks to Professor Moriarty, Gerald Atterleigh will no longer threaten anyone on this earth,' Mrs. Atterleigh said. 'And I pity the denizens of Hell that must deal with him.'

Moriarty let go of Mrs. Atterleigh's hands, looking self-conscious for the first time since I had known him. 'It was an interesting problem,' he said.

Mrs. Atterleigh went to the sideboard and took a decanter from the tantalus. 'It is not too early, I think, for a glass of port,' she said, looking questioningly at us.

'Thank you, but we cannot stay,' Moriarty said.

'A small glass,' she said, pouring the umber liquid into three small stemmed glasses and handing us each one.

Moriarty took a sip, and then another, and then stared down at his glass. 'My God!' he said. 'This is the '09 Languert D'or! I didn't know there was any of this left in the world.'

'I have a new gentleman friend,' she

said. 'His cellars, I believe, are unrivaled. Now, what can I do for you, my dear Professor?'

'Vincent Tams, the newly-defunct Earl of Whitton,' Moriarty said. 'Do you know of him?'

'He died at the Paradol Club last week,' Mrs. Atterleigh said. 'I believe he was alone in bed at the time, which was unlike him.'

'He was a regular visitor to the *demi-monde?*'

'Say rather he dwelled in its precincts,' Mrs. Atterleigh said.

Moriarty turned to me. 'Mrs. Atterleigh is my gazette to the *fils du joi* — the harlots, strumpets and courtesans of London,' he said. 'They all trust her, and bring her their problems. And on occasion, when it violates no confidences, she passes on information to me.'

I remained silent and sipped my port.

'Was his lordship keeping a mistress?' Moriarty asked.

'Always,' Mrs. Atterleigh replied. 'He changed them every three or four months, but he was seldom without.'

'Do you know who was the current inamorata at the time of his death?'

'Lenore,' she said. 'Dark-haired, slender, exotic looking, artistic; she is, I believe, from Bath.'

'Will she speak with me?' Moriarty asked.

'I'll give you a note,' Mrs. Atterleigh said. 'I would come with you, but I'm expecting company momentarily.'

Moriarty rose to his feet. 'Then we will not keep you. If you would be so kind — '

Mrs. Atterleigh went to her writing-desk and composed a brief note, which she handed to Moriarty. 'I have written the address on the outside,' she said. 'Please come back to see me soon, when you don't have to run off.'

'I shall,' Moriarty said.

She turned to me and stretched out a hand. 'Mr. Barnett,' she said. 'You are welcome here, too. Any time. Please visit.'

'I would be honored,' I said.

We left the house and walked down the street to hail a cab. As the vehicle took us back up the street again, I saw a black covered carriage stop in front of the house we had just left. A man in formal attire got out and went up the steps. Just as we passed he turned around to say something to his driver and I got a good look at his face. 'Moriarty!' I said. 'That was the prime minister!'

'Ah, well,' Moriarty said. 'He is reputed to have an excellent wine cellar.'

The address we went to was in a mews off St. Humbert's Square. A small woman with raven-black hair, bright dark eyes, and a cheerful expression threw the door open at our ring. She was wearing a painter's smock, and by the daubs of color on it I judged that the garment had seen its intended use. 'Well?' she demanded.

'Miss Lenore Lestrelle?' Moriarty asked.

She looked us up and down, and didn't seem impressed by what she saw. 'I have enough insurance,' she said, 'I don't read books, and if a distant relative died and left me a vast fortune which you will procure for me for only a few pounds for your out-of-pocket expenses, I'm not interested, thank you very much. Does that cover it?'

Moriarty handed her the note and she read it thoughtfully and then stepped aside. 'Come in then.'

She led us down a hallway to a long room at the rear, which had been fixed up as an artist's studio. An easel holding a large canvas on which paint had begun to be blocked in faced us as we entered the room. On a platform under the skylight a thin red-headed woman, draped in artfully arranged bits of gauze, stood with a Greek urn balanced on her shoulder.

'Take a break, Mollie,' Miss Lestrelle said. 'These gentleman want to talk to me.'

Mollie jumped off the platform and pulled a housecoat around her shoulders. 'I'll be in the kitchen then, getting summat to eat,' she said. 'Call me when you need me.'

A large wooden table piled high with stacks of books and clothing and assorted household goods stood against one wall, surrounded by similarly burdened straight back chairs. Miss Lestrelle waved in their general direction. 'Take your coats off. Sit if you like,' she said. 'Just pile the stuff on the floor.'

'That's all right, Miss Lestrelle,' Moriarty said.

'Suit yourself,' she said. 'Don't bother with the 'Miss Lestrelle.' Lenore is good enough.'

'My name is Professor Moriarty, and this is Mr. Barnett,' Moriarty told her.

'So the letter said. And you want to know about Vincent. Why?'

'We are enquiring into his death.'

'I can't be much help to you there. I didn't see him for several days before he died.'

'I thought he was — ah — '

'Keeping me? That he was. In a nice flat in as fashionable a section of town as is reasonable in the circumstances.' She waved a hand at the goods piled up on the table. 'Those are my things from there. I've just finished moving out.'

'Ah!' Moriarty said. 'The brother evicted you?'

'I've not seen the brother. This is where I do my work, and this is where I choose to be. I am an artist by choice and a harlot only by necessity. As there was no longer any reason to remain in that flat, I left.'

A fair number of canvases were leaning stacked against the near wall, and Moriarty started flipping them forward and examining them one at a time. 'You don't seem overly broken up at his lordship's death,' he commented.

Lenore turned, her hands on her hips, and glared at Moriarty. After a moment she shrugged and sat on a high wooden stool by her easel. 'It was not a love match,' she said. 'Most men want their mistresses to provide love and affection, but Vincent wanted only one thing of his women: to be there when he called. He was not particularly faithful to the girl he was keeping at the moment, and he tired of her after a few months. As I'd been with Vincent for over three months, I expected to be replaced within the fortnight. The flat he kept, the girls were transitory.'

'You had to be at the flat all day waiting for him?'

'After ten at night,' she said. 'If he

hadn't found another interest by ten or eleven, he wanted to have someone to come home to.'

'Did he ever discuss his business affairs with you?'

'Never.'

'Ever have any visitors?'

'Once we had another girl in for the evening, but aside from that none.'

'How did you feel about that?'

Lenore shrugged. 'He was paying the bills,' she said.

Moriarty looked up from his study of the paintings. 'How would you describe his sexual tastes? You can speak freely. Mr. Barnett is a journalist, and therefore unshockable.'

'I have no objection to talking about it if you have no objection to listening. Lord Tams was normal that way. No strange desires or positions or partners. He was just rather insistent. He felt that if he didn't bed a woman every night he would die.'

I couldn't help but exclaim, 'Every night?'

'So he told me.' She looked at me.

'You're trying to solve his murder?'

'That's right,' I said.

She turned to Moriarty. 'And you're Professor Moriarty. I've heard of you. Then I guess it's all right.'

Moriarty leaned forward like a hound dog catching a scent. 'What's all right?' he asked her.

'Talking about Vincent. A person in my trade shouldn't talk about her clients, it isn't professional. And since I haven't found a patron for my art yet, I can't afford to take my departure from the sporting life.'

'Has anyone else asked you to talk about Vincent?' Moriarty asked.

'Oh, no,' she said. 'Not specifically. But there's always men wanting to hear about other men. I figure there's men who like to do it, men who like to talk about doing it, and men who like to hear about it. They come around and buy a girl dinner and ask all sorts of questions about who does what and what other men like to do and what do girls really like, and that sort of thing. Most of them claim to be writers, but I never heard of them. And where could they publish the stories I tell them?'

'The intimate tastes of men are varied, and stretch from the mundane to the absurd,' Moriarty commented.

'I'll say,' Lenora agreed. 'Why I could tell you — ' She smiled. 'But I won't. Except about poor Vincent, which is why you're here.'

'Indeed,' Moriarty agreed. 'So Vincent saw his prowess as necessary to his health?'

'That he did. About three weeks ago, when for a couple of nights he couldn't — perform — he went into a sulk like you've never seen. I tried cheering him up, told him he was just overtired, or ill, and would be up to snuff in no time.'

'How did he take to your cheering words?' Moriarty asked.

'He threw a fit. I thought he had gone crazy. He broke everything in the house that could be lifted, and some that couldn't. He knocked me down, but that was an accident. I got between him and something he was trying to break. When everything was broken, he collapsed on the floor. The next morning when he left he seemed quite normal, as if nothing had happened. That afternoon a team of men from Briggs and Mendel came to repair the damage and replace the furniture and crockery.'

'And how was he after that?'

'I only saw him a couple of times after that. Once he came to the flat, and once he sent a carriage for me to join him at the Paradol Club. There's an inconspicuous door around the side for the special friends of the members. He was unusually silent, but he had recovered from his trouble, whatever it was. He proved that.'

'Did you notice any peculiar bruises on his body when you saw him?'

'Bruises? Why, yes. On his neck. Two bright red marks, almost opposite each other. I asked him about them, and he laughed and said something about Shelley.'

'Shelley?' I asked. 'The poet?'

'I suppose. He said something about an homage to Shelley, and then for a long time we didn't speak. And then I left, and that was the last time I saw him.'

'I see you're heavily influenced by the French school,' Moriarty said.

'Excuse me?'

'Your art.' Moriarty gestured toward the paintings. 'You're quite good.'

'Oh. Thank you.'

'Will you sell me one?'

'Will I — you don't have to — '

'I want to. I'll tell you what; there's a gentleman who owns an art gallery in the Strand who owes me a favor. I'll send him down to see you, look at your work.'

'That would be very kind.'

'Nonsense. After he's seen your stuff he'll owe me two favors. We'll have to make up some tale about your past, London society is not ready for a harlot artist. It's barely ready for a woman artist. You won't make as much money as men who only paint half as well, but it'll be better than you're doing now.'

Lenore had the wide-eyed look of a poor little girl at the pastry counter. 'I don't know what to say,' she said.

'Say nothing until it happens,' Moriarty said. 'And I'll be back next week to pick out a painting for myself.'

'Whichever you want, it's yours,' Lenore said.

'We'll let Vincent's brother pay for it,' Moriarty said. It's only fitting.' He took her hand. 'It's been a pleasure meeting you,' he said. 'You've been a great help.'

We exited to the street, leaving behind a pleased Miss Lestrelle. 'Moriarty,' I said, putting my collar up against the light drizzle that had begun while we were inside, 'you shouldn't do that.'

'What?'

'You know perfectly well what. Raising that girl's hopes like that. I got a good look at her paintings and they were nothing but blobs of color splattered on the canvas. Why, from close up you almost couldn't tell what the pictures represented.'

Moriarty laughed. 'Barnett,' he said, 'you are a fixed point of light in an otherwise hazy world. Just trust me that Van Delding will not consider himself ill used to look at those canvases. The world of art has progressed in the last few decades, along with practically everything else. And we are going to have to accustom ourselves to even more rapid changes in the future.'

'I hope you're wrong,' I told him. 'Few of the changes that I've observed over the last quarter-century have been for the better.'

'Change is the natural condition of life,' Moriarty said. 'Stones do not change of themselves.' He hailed a passing hansom cab and gave our address to the driver. 'Well, Barnett,' he said as we started off, 'what do you think?'

'I think I've missed my lunch,' I said.

'True,' he admitted. 'I get rather single-minded when I'm concentrating on a problem.' He knocked on the roof and shouted to the driver to change our destination to the Savoy.

'I don't see as we're any further along with discovering how Lord Tams met his death,' I told him. 'We've learned a lot about the character and habits of the deceased earl, but it doesn't seem to have gotten us any closer to the way he died.'

Moriarty glanced at me. 'Scientists must train themselves to use rational deductive processes in solving whatever problems come their way, whether they involve distant galaxies or sordid crimes in Belgravia,' he said. 'And the deductive process begins with the collection of data. Only after we have all the facts can we separate the dross from the gold.'

'Of course, Moriarty,' I said. 'And what of this case? You must have some facts that are relevant to the problem at hand on which to set those rational processes to work. Lord Vincent Tams may have been a sexual glutton, but I fail to see how a knowledge of his grosser appetites of the flesh will advance our knowledge of how he died.'

'Grosser appetites of the flesh?' Moriarty said. 'Very good, Barnett; you outdo yourself. If you reflect on what we have learned these past few hours, you will realize that our time has not entirely been wasted.'

'I am not aware that we have learned anything of value,' I said.

Moriarty considered for a moment. 'We have learned that the defunct earl spoke of Shelley,' he said, 'and that by itself should tell us all. But we have learned more: We have learned that artistic talent can flower in the most unlikely places.'

'Flower!' I said. 'Pah!'

Moriarty looked at me. 'Who, for example, would suspect that such fine writing talent could emerge from a quondam reporter for the New York World?'

'Pah!' I repeated.

I had some errands that occupied me after lunch, and Moriarty was out when I returned to Russell Square. I dined alone, and was catching up on filing some accumulated newspaper clippings when the door to the study was flung open and a tall man with a scraggly beard, a dark, well-patched overcoat, and a blue cap strode in. Convinced that I was being accosted by a dangerous anarchist, I rose, trying to remember where I had put my revolver.

'Ah, Barnett,' the anarchist said in the most familiar voice I know, 'I hope there is some dinner left. I have been forced to drink more than I should of a variety of vile liquors, and I didn't trust the food.'

'Moriarty!' I exclaimed. 'I will ring for

cook to prepare something at once. Where have you been?'

'Patience,' Moriarty said, taking off his long gabardine overcoat. He pulled off the beard and reached into his mouth to remove two gutta-percha pads from his cheeks. Then a few quick swipes over his face with a damp sponge, and he was once again recognizable. 'Food first, and perhaps a cup of coffee. Then I'll tell you of my adventures.'

I rang and told the girl to have cook prepare a tray for the professor, and she returned with it inside of five minutes. Moriarty ate rapidly, seemingly unaware of what he was eating, his eyes fixed on the far wall. I had seen these symptoms before. He was working out some problem, and I knew better than to interrupt. If it was a difficult one he might spend hours, or even days, with a pencil and note-pad in front of him, drinking countless cups of coffee and consuming quantities of the rough-cut Virginia tobacco he favored in one of his briar pipes, and staring off into space before he again became conscious of his surroundings.

But this time the problem had worked itself out by the time he finished the last of the roast, and he poured himself a small glass of cognac and waved the bottle in my direction. 'This was laid in the cask twenty years before we met,' he said, 'and it has aged well. Let me pour you a dram!'

'Not tonight, Moriarty,' I said. 'Tell me what you have discovered!'

'Ah!' he said. 'There was a fact in the new Earl of Whitton's statement to us that begged for examination, and I have spent the afternoon and evening examining it.'

'What fact?' I asked.

'How many clubs are you a member of, my friend?'

I thought for a second. 'Let's see . . . The Century, the American Service Club, Whites, the Bellona; that's it at present.'

'And you have, no doubt, an intimate knowledge of two or three others through guest membership, or visiting friends and the like?'

'I suppose so.'

'And of these half-dozen clubs you are well acquainted with, how many have club doctors?'

'I'm sure they all have physician members,' I said.

'Your reasoning is impeccable,' Moriarty said. 'But how many of them have doctors on staff?'

'Why, none,' I said. 'Why would a club keep a doctor on staff?'

'My question exactly,' Moriarty said. 'But Dr. Papoli was described by both Lord Tams and Inspector Lestrade as the club doctor, which implies a professional relationship between the doctor and the club. And a further question: if, for some reason, the directors of a club decided to hire a doctor, would they pick one who, as Lord Tams told us, lacks a British medical degree?'

'Certainly not!' I said.

'Quite so. And so I went to that area of the East End that is teaming with Balkan immigrants and I let it be known that I was in search of a doctor. I hinted at mysterious needs, but I was very vague, since I didn't know just what the needs in question were.'

'But Moriarty,' I said, 'You don't speak the language.'

'There are five or six possible languages,' Moriarty said. 'Whenever someone spoke to me in anything other than English, I told him I was from Ugarte, and didn't understand his dialect.'

'Where is Ugarte?' I asked.

'I have no idea,' Moriarty said. 'I would be very surprised if there is any such place.'

'What did you find out?' I asked.

'That Dr. Papoli is looked upon with almost superstitious dread by his country-men, and that he has recently hired several assistants with strong backs and dubious reputations.'

'And what does that tell you?'

'That a visit to the Paradol Club is in order for tomorrow. But for now I will enjoy my cognac, and then get a good night's sleep.'

Although it was clear that Moriarty had reached some conclusion, he did not share it with me. That night I dreamed of beautiful women in *dishabille* marching on Parliament and demanding the right to paint. The prime minister and Beatrice were singing a duet from *Pirates of Penzance* to a packed House of Commons, who were about to join in on the chorus, when the chimes on my alarm clock woke me up the next morning.

The Paradol Club was housed in a large building at the corner of Montague and Charles Streets. The brass plaque on the front door was very small and discreet, and the ground floor windows were all barred. Moriarty and I walked around the block twice, Moriarty peering at windows and poking at the pavement and the buildings with his walking stick. There appeared to be two additional entrances; a small, barred door on Charles Street, and an alleyway leading to a rear entry. After the second circuit we mounted the front steps and entered the club.

Considering what we had been told of the Paradol Club, the entrance area was disappointingly mundane. To the right was a cloakroom and porter's room; to the left was the manager's office, with a desk by the door. Past the desk was the door to the front reading-room, with a rack holding current newspapers and magazines visible inside. A little bird-like man sitting behind the desk leaned forward and cocked his head to the side as we entered. 'Gentlemen,' he said. 'Welcome to the Paradol Club. Of which of our members are you the guests?'

'Are you the club manager?'

'I am the assistant manager, Torkson by name.'

Moriarty nodded. 'I am Professor Moriarty,' he said. 'I am here to investigate the death of one of your members. This is my associate, Mr. Barnett.'

Torkson reared back as though he had been stung. 'Which one?' he asked.

'How many have there been?' Moriarty asked.

'Three in the past three months,' Torkson said. 'Old General Quincy, Hapsman the barrister, and Lord Tams.'

'It is the death of Vincent Tams that occupies us at the moment,' Moriarty said. 'Has his room been cleaned out yet, and if not may we see it?'

'Who sent you?' Torkson asked.

'Lord Tams,' Moriarty said.

Torkson looked startled. 'The Lord Tams that is,' explained Moriarty, 'has asked me to enquire into the death of the Lord Tams that was.'

'Ah!' said Torkson. 'That would be Mr. Everett. Well then, I guess it will be all right.' Pulling a large ring of keys from a desk drawer, he led the way upstairs. 'Lord Tams kept a room here permanently,' he said. 'Our hostesses were very fond of him, as he was always a perfect gentleman and very generous,' he added, pausing on the first floor landing and glancing back at us. Moriarty and I just stared back at him, as though the idea of 'hostesses' at a gentleman's club were perfectly normal. Reassured, he took us up to the second floor, and down the hall to Vincent Tams's room. Again I was struck by the very normality of my surroundings. One would expect a club defined by its members' addiction to vice, as others are by their members' military backgrounds or fondness for cricket, to have risqué wall hangings or scantily clad maidens dashing from room to room. But from the dark wood furniture to the paintings of hunting scenes on the wall, it all looked respectable, mundane, and very British.

When we reached the door to Vincent Tams's room the assistant manager paused and turned to us. 'Do you suppose the new Lord Tams will wish to keep the room?' he asked.

'He is hoping to get married in the near future,' I said.

'Ah!' said Torkson. 'Then he will almost certainly wish to keep the room.' He unlocked the door and turned to go.

'One moment,' Moriarty said. 'Is the waiter who found his lordship's body available?'

'Williamson,' the assistant manager said. 'I believe he is working today.'

'Will you please send him up here?'

Torkson nodded and scurried off back downstairs. The room was actually a three-room suite. Moriarty and I entered a sitting room, to the left was the bedroom, and to the right a small dining room. The sitting room was fixed with a writing desk, a couch and an easy chair. A large bookcase took up one wall. Moriarty whipped out a magnifying glass and tape measure and began a methodical examination of the walls and floor.

'What can I do, Professor?' I asked.

He thought for a second. 'Examine the books,' he said.

'For what?' I asked.

'Anything that isn't book,' he told me.

I went to the bookcase and took down some of the volumes at random. Except for some popular novels and a six-volume work on the Napoleonic Wars, they were all books that could not be displayed in mixed company. Most were what are called 'French' novels, and the rest were full of erotic drawings displaying couples coupling, many in positions that I had never dreamed of, and some in positions that I believe are impossible to attain. I began going through them methodically, right to left, top to bottom, for anything that might have been inserted between the pages, but found nothing.

There was a knock at the door and I

turned to see a thickset man in the uniform of a waiter standing in the doorway. 'You wished to see me, sir?' he asked, addressing the air somewhere between Moriarty and myself.

'Williamson?' Moriarty asked.

'That's right, sir.'

'You found Lord Tams's body the morning he died?'

'I did, sir, and quite a shock it was too.' Williamson stepped into the room and closed the door.

'Tell me,' Moriarty said.

'Well, sir, I brought the tray up at a quarter to eight, as instructed, and entered the sitting room.'

'You had a key?'

'Yes, sir. I got the key from the porter on the way up. My instructions were to set breakfast up in the dining room, and then to knock on the bedroom door at eight o'clock sharp. Which same I did. Only there was no answer.'

'One breakfast or two?' Moriarty asked.

'Only one.'

'Was that usual?'

'Oh yes, sir. If a hostess spent the night

with his lordship, she left when he sat down to breakfast.'

'I see,' said Moriarty. 'And when there was no answer?'

'I waited a moment and then knocked again. Getting no response, I ventured to open the door.'

'And?'

'There was his lordship, lying face-up on the bed, staring at the ceiling. His hands were raised in the air over his head, as though he were afraid someone were going to hit him. His face were beet-red. He were dead.'

'Were the bed-clothes covering him?'

'No, sir. He were lying atop of them.'

'What did you do?'

'I chucked.'

'You — ?'

'I threw up. All over my dickey, too.'

'Very understandable. And then?'

'And then I went downstairs and told Mr. Caltro, the manager. And he fetched Dr. Papoli, and I went to the pantry to change my dickey.'

Moriarty pulled a shilling out of his pocket and tossed it to the waiter. 'Thank you, Williamson,' he said. 'You've been quite helpful.'

'Thank you, sir,' Williamson said, pocketing the coin and leaving the room.

A short, dapper man with a spade beard that looked as if it belonged on a larger face knocked on the open door, took two steps into the room, and bowed. The tail of his black frock coat bobbed up as he bent over, giving the impression that one was observing a large, black fowl. 'Professor Moriarty?' he asked.

Moriarty swiveled to face the intruder. 'That is I.'

'Ah! Torkson told me you were here. I am Dr. Papoli. Can I be of any service to you?'

'Perhaps. What can you tell me of Lord Tams's death?'

Dr. Papoli shrugged. 'When I was called he had been dead for several hours. Rigor was pronounced. His face was flushed, which suggested to me the apoplexy; but I was overruled by the superior knowledge of your British doctors. If you would know more, you had best ask them.'

'I see,' Moriarty said. 'Thank you, doctor.'

Papoli bowed and backed out of the room.

Moriarty crossed to the bedroom and gazed at the rumpled bedclothes. 'Picture it, Barnett,' he said. 'The dead earl staring up at the ceiling, his face unnaturally red and bearing a horrified expression, his arms raised against an unseen foe. And the strange puncture marks on the body, don't leave those out of your picture.' He turned to me. 'What does that image convey to you?'

'Something frightful must have happened in this room,' I said, 'but what the nature of that happening was, I have no idea.'

Moriarty shook his head. 'Nothing frightful happened in this room,' he said. 'Understanding that will give you the key to the mystery.' He took one last look around the room and then went out into the hall. For the next half hour he walked up and down the hallway on that floor and the ones above and below, peering and measuring. Finally he returned to where I awaited him on the second floor landing. 'Come,' he said.

'Where?'

'Back to Russell Square.'

We left the club and flagged down a hansom. Moriarty was taciturn and seemed distracted on the ride home. When we entered the house, Moriarty put a small blue lantern in the window; the sign to any passing members of the Mendicants' Guild that they were wanted. Moriarty has a long-standing relationship with the Mendicants' Guild and Twist, their leader. They are his eyes all over London, and he supplies them with technical advice of a sort they cannot get from more usual sources. About half an hour later a leering hunchback with a grotesquely flattened nose knocked on the door. 'My moniker's Handsome Bob,' he told Moriarty when he was brought into the office, 'Twist sent me.'

'Here's your job,' Moriarty told the beggar. 'The Paradol Club is at the intersection of Montague and Charles. It has three entrances. Most people use the main entrance on Montague Street. I want a watch kept on the club, and I want the men to give me the best description they can of anyone who enters the club through either of the other two entrances. But without drawing any attention to themselves. Send someone to report to me every half-hour, but keep the place covered at all times.'

'Yessir, Professor Moriarty,' Handsome Bob said, touching his hand to his cap. 'Four of the boys should be enough. We'll get right on it.'

Moriarty reached into the apothecary jar on the mantle and took out a handful of coins. 'Have them return here by cab if there's anything interesting to report,' he said, handing the coins to Bob. 'This is for current expenses. I'll settle with you at the usual rates after.'

'Yessir, Professor Moriarty,' Handsome Bob repeated, and he turned and sidled out the door.

Moriarty turned to me. 'Now we wait,' he said.

'What are we waiting for?'

'For the villain to engage in his employment,' Moriarty said. He leaned back and settled down to read the latest copy of the quarterly *Journal of the British Geological Society*. I left the room and took a long walk, stopping for sustenance at a local pub, which I find soothes my mind.

I returned at about six in the evening, and stretched out on the sitting room couch to take a nap. It was just after eleven when Moriarty shook me by the shoulder. Standing behind him was an emaciated-looking man on crutches, a crippled beggar I remembered seeing at Twist's headquarters in a Godolphin Street warehouse. 'Quick, Barnett,' Moriarty cried, 'our drama has taken a critical turn. Get your revolver while I hail a cab!' He grabbed his hat, stick, and overcoat and was out the door in an instant.

I ran upstairs to my bedroom and pulled my revolver from its drawer, made sure it was loaded, and then grabbed my overcoat and ran downstairs. Moriarty had stopped two cabs, and was just finishing scribbling a note on the back of an envelope. He handed the note to the beggar. 'Give this to Inspector Lestrade, and no one else,' he said. 'He will be waiting for you.'

Moriarty put the cripple in the first cab and looked up at the driver. 'Take this man to Scotland Yard, and wait for him,' he said. 'And hurry!'

We climbed into the second cab together and set off at a good pace for the Paradol Club. Moriarty leaned forward impatiently in his seat. 'This is devilish,' he said. 'I never anticipated this.'

'What, Moriarty, for God's sake?'

'Two people of interest have entered the back door of the club in the past hour,' he said. 'One was a young girl of no particular status who was taken in by two burly men and looked frightened to the watcher. The other was the Duke of Claremore.'

'Moriarty!' I said. 'But he's — '

'Yes,' Moriarty agreed. 'And we must put an end to this quickly, quietly, and with great care. If it were ever to become known that a royal duke was involved — '

'Put an end to what?' I asked. 'Just what is going on in the Paradol Club?'

Moriarty turned to look at me. 'The

Greeks called it hubris,' he said.

We arrived at the club and jumped from the cab. 'Wait around the corner!' Moriarty yelled at the driver as we raced up the front steps. The door was closed but the porter, a thickset man with the look of a retired sergeant of marine, answered our knock after a few seconds, pulling his jacket on as he opened the door. Moriarty grabbed him by the collar. 'Listen, man,' he said. 'Several detectives from Scotland Yard will arrive here any minute. Stay out front and wait for them. When they arrive, direct them to Dr. Papoli's consulting room on the second floor. Tell them that I said to be very quiet and not to disturb any of the other guests.'

'And who are you?' the porter asked.

'Professor James Moriarty.' And Moriarty left the porter in the doorway and raced up the stairs, with me close behind.

The second floor corridor was dark, and we moved along it by feel, running our hands along the wall as we went. 'Here,' Moriarty said. 'This should be the doctor's door.' He put his ear to the door, and then tried the handle. 'Damn — it's locked.'

A match flared, and the light steadied, and I saw that Moriarty had lighted a plumber's candle that he took from his pocket. 'Hold this for me, will you?' he asked.

Moriarty handed me the candle and took a small, curved implement from his pocket. He inserted it into the lock and, after a few seconds fiddling, the door opened. We entered a large room, which was dark and deserted. I held up the candle, and we could see a desk and couch, and a row of cabinets along one wall.

'There should be a staircase in here somewhere,' Moriarty said running his hand along the molding on the far wall.

'A staircase?' I asked.

'Yes. I measured the space when we were here earlier, and an area just below this room has been closed off, with no access from that floor. Also water has recently been laid on in this corner of the building and a drain put in. You can see the pipes hugging the wall from outside.

Logic says that — aha!'

There was a soft click and a section of the wall swung open on silent hinges, revealing a narrow stairs going down. A brilliant shaft of light from below illuminated the staircase.

Moriarty, his revolver drawn, crept down the staircase, and I was but a step behind him. The sight that greeted my eyes as the room below came into view was one that will stay with me forever. It was as though I was witness to a scene from one of *Le Grand Guignol*'s dramas of horror, but the chamber below me was not a stage setting, and the people were not actors.

The room was an unrelieved white, from the painted walls to the tile floor, and a pair of calcium lights mounted on the ceiling eliminated all shadow and cast an unnatural brightness over the scene. Two metal tables of the sort used in operating theatres stood several feet apart in the middle of the room. Surrounding them was a madman's latticework of tubing, piping, and glassware, emanating from a machine that squatted between the two tables, the purpose of which I could not even begin to guess.

On the table to my right, partially covered by a sheet, lay an elderly man; on the other table a young girl similarly covered had been tied down by leather straps. Both were unconscious, with ether cones covering their nose and mouth. Between them stood Dr. Papoli, his black frock coat replaced by a white surgical apron, absorbed in his task of inserting a thin cannula into the girl's thigh. His assistant, also in white, was swabbing an area on the man's thigh with something that left a brown stain.

'All right, doctor,' Moriarty said, starting toward the tables. 'I think it would be best if you stopped right now!'

Papoli looked up, an expression of annoyance on his face. 'You mustn't interrupt!' he said. 'You will ruin the experiment.'

'Your experiments have already ruined too many people,' Moriarty said, raising his revolver. 'Get away from the girl! The police will be here any second.'

Papoli cursed in some foreign language

and, grabbing a brown bottle, threw it violently against the wall. It shattered and, in an instant, a sickly-sweet smell filled the room, a smell I recognized from some dental surgery I'd had the year before.

'Don't shoot, Professor!' I yelled. 'It's ether! One shot could blow us all into the billiard room!'

'Quick!' Moriarty said, 'we must get the duke and the girl out of here.'

Papoli and his assistant were already halfway up the stair. Doing my best to hold my breath, I staggered over to the tables. Moriarty lifted the duke onto his shoulders, and I unstrapped the girl and grabbed her, I'm not sure how, and headed for the stairs.

While we were on the staircase two shots rang out from the room above, and I heard the sound of a scuffle. We entered the room to find Lestrade glaring at the doctor and his assistant, who were being firmly held by two large policemen. 'He shot at me, Moriarty, can you believe that?' Lestrade said, sounding thoroughly annoyed. 'Now, what have we here?'

We lay our burdens gently on the floor, and I stanched the wound on the girl's thigh with my cravat.

Moriarty indicated the unconscious man on the floor. 'This is the Duke of Claremore,' he said. 'It would be best to get him out of here before his presence becomes known. Dr. Papoli can safely be charged with murder, and his accomplice, I suppose, with being an accomplice. We'll see that the girl is cared for. Come to Russell Square tomorrow at noon, and I'll explain all over lunch.'

'But Moriarty — '

'Not now, Lestrade. Tomorrow.'

'Oh, very well,' Lestrade said. He turned to a policeman by the door. 'Get a chair to seat his lordship in, and we'll carry him downstairs,' he instructed.

We took the waiting cab to Abelard Court, and Beatrice Atterleigh herself opened the door to our knock. She did not seem surprised to find us standing at her door supporting a barely-conscious girl at one in the morning.

'Will you take care of this girl for a few days?' Moriarty asked. 'She has been mistreated. I have no idea what language she speaks.'

'Of course,' Mrs. Atterleigh said.

The next morning at quarter to twelve our client arrived at Russell Square in response to a telegram. Lestrade arrived at noon sharp, thereby demonstrating the punctuality of the detective police.

We sat down to duckling à l'orange and an '82 Piesporter, and Moriarty regaled us with a discourse on wines through the main course. It was not until the serving girl put the trifle on the table and Moriarty had poured us each a small glass of the Imperial Tokay — from a case presented to Moriarty by Franz Joseph himself upon the successful conclusion of a problem involving the chief of the *Kundschafts Stelle* and a ballerina — that he was willing to talk about the death of Lord Vincent Tams.

'It was obvious from the start,' Moriarty began, 'that Lord Tams did not die where he was found. Which raised the questions why was he moved, and from where?'

'Obvious to you, perhaps,' Lestrade said.

'Come now,' Moriarty said. 'His hands were raised and his face was flushed. But corpses do not lie with their hands raised, nor with their faces flushed.'

'This one did,' Lestrade said. 'I saw it.'

'You saw it full in the grip of rigor mortis,' Moriarty said, 'which makes the body rigid in whatever position it has assumed. But how did it assume that position? The face gives it away. The head was lower than the body after death.'

'Of course!' I said. 'Lividity. I should have known.'

'Lividity?' Lord Tams asked.

'After death the blood pools at the body's lowest point,' I told him, 'which makes the skin in that area appear red. I've seen it many times as a reporter on the New York police beat. I'm just not used to hearing of it on faces.'

'Your brother was at the Paradol Club to avail himself of the services of Dr. Papoli,' Moriarty said, turning in his chair to face Lord Tams. 'The doctor claimed to have a method to rejuvenate a man's lost vitality. He transfused his patients with youthful blood. Thus they regained youthful vigor. It is a not uncommon desire of men, as they get older, to recapture their youth. Papoli was preying on men who could afford to attempt it. Occasionally one of his patients died, because for some reason as yet unknown, some people's blood will cause a fatal reaction when injected into another. Papoli claimed that he had devised a machine that would solve that problem — the strange apparatus that was between the two beds. But he was obviously mistaken.'

'How do you know that?' Lestrade asked.

'I went to talk to your prisoner this morning,' Moriarty said. He is extremely indignant that he is in jail. He considers himself a savior of man. He is quite mad.'

'So other men died besides my brother?' Lord Tams asked.

'Yes, several. But they were elderly men, and their natural vanity had kept them from telling anyone about the operation, so his secret remained safe.

Occasionally one of his donors died, but they came from the poorest classes of the city and they were not missed.'

'But my brother was not that old.'

'True. It was his obsession with sexual vitality that made him seek the operation. It failed. Papoli and his assistant thought your brother had died on the table. They left him there, not wanting to carry a body through the hallway early in the evening. Later, when they came back to take him to his room, they found that he had briefly regained consciousness and partially removed his restraining straps. The upper half of his body fell off the table in his dying convulsions, and he was left hanging from a strap around his legs. That explains his hands, which had fallen toward the floor. When they lifted him, rigor had set in and his arms looked as though they were raised.'

Lord Tams sighed. 'Poor Vincent.' He stood up. 'Well, Professor Moriarty, you have saved my marriage, and possibly my life. I had the impression that Inspector Lestrade was preparing to clap me in irons at any second.'

'That's as it may be,' Lestrade said. 'No hard feelings, I trust?'

'None, Inspector. I invite you — all of you — to my wedding. I must be off now to see Miss Whitsome and tell her the happy news. Professor Moriarty, you will send me a bill, whatever you think is right, and I will pay it promptly, I assure you.'

Moriarty nodded, and Lord Tams clapped his bowler on his head and was out the door. A minute later Lestrade followed.

'Moriarty,' I said, refilling my coffee cup, 'two last questions.'

Moriarty held out his own cup for a refill. 'What?' he asked.

'Do you think the new Lord Tams will keep his brother's rooms at the Paradol?'

'I never speculate,' Moriarty said, 'it is bad for the deductive process.' He leaned back. 'But if I were a betting man, I'd put a tenner on it. What else?'

'Miss Lestrelle told us that Vincent had made some reference to Shelley, and you said that that told all. Were you serious? I looked through my copy of Shelley this morning, and I could find nothing that applies.'

Moriarty smiled. 'I fancy you were looking up the wrong Shelley,' he said.

'The wrong — '

Moriarty reached over to the bookshelf and tossed a book across to me. 'Try this one.'

I looked down at the book. On the cover, in an ornate Gothic type, was the title: *Frankenstein, or The Modern Prometheus*, by Mary Wollstonecraft Shelley.

Moriarty was out all this morning, and he came back with a painting by Lenore Lestrelle. It is all green and brown and blue blotches and seems to be some sort of pastoral scene. I am afraid that he intends to hang it in the dining room.

4

The Picture of Oscar Wilde

I make no apologies for what follows, it begins. *It is my intention that none shall read these words for the next — let us say — 100 years. But that is not as much out of the well of modesty for which I am widely known and justly admired; but from a desire that I shall trouble no one with my peccadilloes, and no one shall trouble me with their approbation. I am quite able to disapprove of myself without outside assistance.*

There it breaks off. Below it on the page are a few random thoughts.

Without the approbation of one's friends where would one be?
And:

One lives for joy and wit and friendship

— but I can't make out what one dies for.

These words are on the first page of an otherwise pristine notebook on the cover of which is printed 'OFOW January 91.'

The playwright, poet, novelist and gadfly Oscar Fingal O'Flahertie Wilde left the notebook in my house sometime during the second week in, as it happens, January of 1891. He never called to reclaim it; perhaps in the flurry of that month's events, he forgot its existence. Perhaps he began again in some other notebook, recounting the events to their sad conclusion, and put the narrative someplace where, in time, his version of the tale will be revealed.

Here is my version.

My name is Benjamin Barnett and I am the proprietor of the North Atlantic Cable News Service, bringing news of Britain and the Continent to North American readers. And I am a friend and erstwhile minion of Professor James Moriarty, who figures largely in this story. The professor rescued me from a Turkish prison some years ago, and in recompense for this service I stayed in his employ for a number of years upon my return to London before establishing the news service.

Oscar Wilde had been writing an irregular column for me on the London theatre scene for the past two years, under the pen name of Fingal Wills. When I asked him why he refused to use his own name, he had told me, 'Writing for the American public is like appearing as the rear end of a musical hall horse. One does it only for the money, and one would as soon not be recognized.' I couldn't argue with him.

It was around eight o'clock on a Tuesday night early in January, if memory serves, when our maid entered my study, where I was going over the accounts of some recent murder trials to see if any might interest a Boston newspaper whose readers seemed to relish British gore. 'That's all right, Tilda,' I told her. 'You can go to bed. I'll turn down the lamps and chivvy my own cup into the pantry.'

'There's a gentleman,' she said. 'At the door.'

'A gentleman?'

'He says he's a gentleman,' she told me, holding out the small silver tray on which rested the gentleman's card.

Oscar Fingal O'Flahertie Wells Wilde

'A gentleman indeed,' I agreed. 'Although what . . . never mind. Show the gentleman in, Tilda, and then you may retire.'

A few moments later Wilde came through the door. His face was paler than usual and his hair was disarranged in an artless manner. 'Thank you for seeing me with no notice,' he said, flopping onto a chair. 'I hope I'm not interrupting anything. Thank God you're home. Your wife — how is your wife?'

'Cecily is upstairs suffering from a headache. She finds both light and sound painful when these come on her, so I try to annoy her as little as possible.'

'Cecily,' he said. 'Lovely name.' He sat bolt upright as though a sudden spasm had gripped his body and an expression of extreme pain — anguish? — flitted across his face. 'Benjamin,' he said, 'you must help me. It is a trick of the gods that I am acquainted with you and that you, I understand, are acquainted with a man named Professor Moriarty.'

'I am,' I said. I was, I confess, puzzled. I could not picture two men less alike than the intense, reserved man of science, Professor James Moriarty, and the mercurial, effervescent, witty aesthete, Oscar Wilde. They both possessed massive intelligence and keen intellects, but they directed these gifts in entirely different directions.

'I must meet him. I must speak with him,' Wilde said. He was tugging at his cravat as though it were the source of his troubles, but he did not seem to notice what he was doing. 'And as soon as possible. The business is private, but urgent. Very urgent. Can you take me to him?'

'Of course.' I considered. 'I'll send him a note first thing in the morning and arrange a meeting.'

'My dear boy,' Wilde said, 'who knows what evils might befall us between now and the morning? Could you not arrange a meeting this evening?'

'Now?' I asked, surprised.

'Why not?' Wilde asked, his voice sharp and anxious. He gestured toward the study window. 'It has stopped snowing, the night is pleasant, the streets are moderately clear. I assure you the need is vital.'

Putting aside my misgivings I gave in to his evident distress and rose from my chair.

'Good, good,' Wilde said. 'Thank you, thank you. I have held my Hansom, which awaits by the door.'

'Then let us go,' I said, shrugging into my jacket. 'If the professor is home, and will see us, we'll be there in ten minutes.'

Wilde retrieved his overcoat, top hat and walking stick from the rack by the door and I assembled my gear from the hall closet and we left. No more than ten minutes later we were knocking on the door of 64 Russell Square. Mr. Maws, Professor Moriarty's butler, admitted us, relieved us of our outerwear, and bade us wait in the front room while he went to see if the professor would receive his unexpected guests.

We had no more than sat down — well, I had sat down and Wilde had commenced pacing back and forth on the oversized Khasmani rug (a gift from the Grand Mufti of Rumelia for an extraordinary — but I digress) — when Professor Moriarty appeared in the doorway. A tall, thin man with a slight forward stoop, as though he were perpetually adjusting to living in a world of people smaller than himself, Moriarty had deep-set dark eyes under heavy brows, giving him the visual aspect of a brooding hawk. One eyebrow was raised quizzically as he looked over his visitors.

'Barnett, what an unexpected pleasure,' he said, stepping into the room. 'And this must be the amazing Mr. Oscar Wilde whom one can't help hearing about wherever one goes in London these days.' He extended his hand. 'It is a pleasure to finally meet you.'

'I fear I cannot shake hands with you, sir,' Wilde said, stepping back from the offered hand and thrusting his own hands theatrically into the pockets of his jacket. 'Mr. Sherlock Holmes has told me all about you!'

'Oh dear,' Moriarty said. 'My own personal Javert is busy again. What slander is he spreading now?'

'His, ah, belief is that you are responsible for all the important crimes committed in London, and for many of the lesser ones,' said Wilde.

'So he has averred to Scotland Yard time and again, and yet I am still here.'

'And that you are most assuredly the mind behind a devious and infernally pernicious plot against me.' Wilde made a vague and somehow plaintive gesture in the air, suddenly looking very tired. 'I come here to find out whether this is true.'

'Ah!' Moriarty said. 'I think I can safely say that it is not. Come into my office, and tell me of just what crime I stand accused.'

We crossed the hall and Moriarty paused to turn up the gas lamps and then settled into the large oak chair behind his massive oak desk and waved us to seats.

Mr. Maws came in behind us bearing a tray holding several cut glass decanters and a gasogene. 'If you'll excuse me, sir,' he said. 'I thought perhaps . . . '

'Yes, of course,' Moriarty said. 'What have you brought us?'

Mr. Maws indicated each decanter in turn. 'O'Brian's Reserve Irish Whiskey,' he said, 'Louis XVII closed cask Cognac, and Port wine Garrafeira, 1826. Just coming into its own, I think.'

'O'Brian's . . . ' Wilde looked interested.

'A good choice sir. And just a splash?' Mr. Maws poured two inches of the golden liquid into a glass, worked the handle of the gasogene to add an equal amount of soda water, and handed the glass to Wilde.

I admitted that the concoction looked good to me, and had one of the same. The professor took a small glass of the port.

'Now,' Moriarty said as Mr. Maws left the room, closing the door gently behind him. 'Tell me the story. I know you suspect me of being intimately involved in it, but relate it as though I know nothing.'

Wilde glared suspiciously at Moriarty, but the glass of Irish whiskey in his hand seemed to reassure him, and sipping at it to fortify him and raise his, if you'll excuse the expression, spirits. 'Blackmail,' he said shortly.

'Ah!' Moriarty replied. 'And in what manner are you being blackmailed?'

Wilde shook his head, his face turning an uncharacteristic red color.

'Surely, sir,' Moriarty said, 'if I'm the one blackmailing you, then I must already know how it's being done. And if I'm not — and I assure you I am not — then perhaps I can help.'

Several emotions, and I am not qualified to say just what they were, but I would judge they were not pleasant, played across Oscar Wilde's face. Then in one gesture he pulled a stiff card from his inner jacket pocket and thrust it toward Moriarty. 'Here,' he said.

Moriarty took the card and, holding it under the lamp on his desk peered at it through a powerful pocket lens, going over it slowly and carefully.

Wilde's manner made it clear that I

would not be welcome to cross to the desk and investigate the item for myself, but I subsequently had the opportunity to examine it closely. It was a photograph of two men reclining on what appeared to be a rug in front of an unlit fireplace. They had no clothes on. Their positions and proximity made them appear to be, shall I say, intimate friends. One of them was Wilde. I trust this is enough of a description to explain the situation without being sufficient to excite pruriency. And to those of you who profess shock at even so brief a description, well, all I can say is that I find your shock suspect and wonder what emotion resides behind it.

'This picture has been staged, I believe,' Moriarty commented.

'Indeed,' Wilde agreed.

'At first I thought that perhaps it was some sort of composite, putting your head on the body of another. But that is difficult to do well, and there is no sign of it here. And the body itself is, ah, identifiable.'

'Yes,' Wilde agreed. 'I'm afraid that,

were I to remove my clothes, there would be little doubt the head is attached to the correct body.' He gave a tired smile. 'Such flaws as are evident cannot in this case be blamed on my tailor.'

'It looks to me as though you have been posed. Were you conscious at the time?'

'As I have no memory of the event, I must assume not,' Wilde told him.

'Do you have any idea when the, ah, event might have occurred?'

Wilde considered. 'Saturday last,' he said. 'I was napping in an office on the second floor of the theater. I awoke several hours later with a violent headache to find my clothing strangely disarranged.'

'What did you think at the time?' I interjected.

Wilde turned to look at me. 'I assumed it was some sort of practical joke. Several of my friends have rather robust senses of humor. I thought this was rather over the top, but I didn't know who to blame or what the intent was — at the time. The next day I received the photograph in the afternoon mail. With it was a very brief note.'

'Ah!' Moriarty said. 'Do you still have the note?'

Wilde took a crumpled piece of paper from his pocket, smoothed it out, and handed it to Moriarty. In large print, which I could easily make out from where I sat, the note said simply:

£10.000

'Succinct,' Moriarty commented.

'I thought so,' Wilde agreed.

'And you have heard nothing further?'

'Not yet.'

'Do you have access to that sort of money?'

'Not if I sell all I own. Not if I sell my soul.'

Moriarty turned to me. 'You see why, Barnett, were I to resort to blackmail, I would not choose artists, writers or actors as my targets. Few of them have sufficient wealth for the project to be worth the effort.' He returned his attention to Wilde. 'Do you know who the other gentleman in the photograph is?'

'His name is Rob Reynard,' Wilde said. 'He is an understudy in the theatrical company that is now putting on a new play of mine. 'Lady Windermere's Fan.' The play is now in rehearsal.'

'And what does he know of this?'

'I have not had the opportunity to speak with him since receiving the picture. He did not appear at rehearsal yesterday or today.'

'Have you actually had any, er, relationship with this young man?' Moriarty asked.

Wilde shook his head. 'Even were I interested in such a liaison, Mr. Reynard is not my type. He's much too earnest a young man. I must have frivolity and clever badinage, and poor Rob seems incapable of either.'

Moriarty thought for a moment. 'Do you have any idea where this photograph was taken?' he asked.

'I believe it's the drawing room set of Lady Windermere,' Wilde said. 'It looks as though we were placed and, ah, arranged on stage.'

'And this stage is?'

'At the St. James Theater.'

Moriarty rose. 'Then let us go forth,' he said. 'I would tread those boards.'

'At this hour?' I asked.

Moriarty pulled out his pocket watch and consulted it. 'It's barely ten o'clock,' he said. 'Surely the theater will still be inhabited.'

'Rehearsals often go on until past midnight,' Wilde affirmed. 'But I trust it won't be necessary to mention why you are there.' I noticed that Wilde had accepted the professor's innocence of involvement without further discussion.

'Of course not,' Moriarty agreed. 'Incidentally, if you went to see Mr. Sherlock Holmes, why did he not take your case?'

'Apparently he believed some of the more outrageous stories about me, even if he wasn't convinced that the photo was genuine.' Wilde said. 'His words were that he doesn't choose to defend immorality.'

'Ever the prig,' Moriarty commented. 'Well, let us be off!'

The rehearsal had ended for the night when we arrived at the theater, and Moriarty had the stage to himself. He spend some time comparing the stage to the photograph, measuring distances and angles with a tape measure and a protractor, and jotting notes and formulas in a small notebook. He had Wilde show him the room from which Wilde had presumably been abducted and he examined the staircase off the front vestibule that led to it.

It was about an hour and a half later when the professor closed his notebook and returned it to his jacket pocket. 'I suggest we adjourn for the night,' he said.

'Have you discovered anything?' asked Wilde.

'I believe I see a course of action that might be not without profit,' Moriarty told him.

'Umph,' said Wilde.

'Be at my house tomorrow at, say, three in the afternoon, and I may have some news for you.'

And we had to be satisfied with that.

I was not sure that I should include myself in the invitation to return to Moriarty's house on the morrow, but Wilde assured me that he desired my continued presence, and so I acquiesced. I confess that I had a strong desire to see the thing through.

Wilde and I showed up at the professor's doorstep within moments of each other at three on Wednesday. Mr. Maws showed us into the professor's office, where we found him behind his desk fiddling with a square black object about the size of a small footstool. 'This is the cause of your troubles,' he told Wilde, placing the object on his desk.

'What is it?' I asked.

'It's the new Baum-Lamphier self-loading camera.' He spun it around and demonstrated. 'Lens here, ground glass viewing screen on the back.' He turned the thing upside-down. 'A film pack of twelve glass plates is loaded in here, and then you turn this lever.' He swung it upright again. 'And now it's loaded and ready to take the first picture. A modern advance in photography which allows the taking of pictures more rapidly if not more artistically.'

'That machine took the photograph?' Wilde asked.

'Well, not this very one, but something very much like it.'

'How do you know that?' I asked.

'There is a slight black bar at the top of Mr. Wilde's photograph,' said Moriarty.

'Not my photograph,' Wilde interjected bitterly.

'Ah, yes. But nonetheless there is the bar. Approximately an eighth of an inch long by a sixteenth of an inch wide, and three-eights of an inch from the top of the photograph on the left-hand side.'

'Not much of a bar,' I opined.

'But sufficient,' Moriarty said. 'Sufficient.'

'What does it signify?' Wilde asked.

'Observe,' Moriarty said, raising the camera. He pointed it toward the window and clicked the shutter. 'Now that one negative plate has been expended,' he said, 'we need to put a new plate in position. But we don't have to remove the used plate first, a process that is time-consuming and destructive of the artistic impulse. Instead — ' Moriarty pulled a lever and turned the camera upside down. A loud click and a soft thud sounded from inside the camera. Moriarty released the lever and righted the camera. '*Voila!* The fresh plate is now in position.'

'Clever,' I said.

'Oh the wonders of modern science,' Wilde said, 'will they never cease?'

'Held in place,' Moriarty continued, 'by a spring and two pins, one on each side of the plate. And, due to what I must assume is a slight but normally unnotice- able manufacturing flaw, the left pin protrudes slightly into the frame of the photograph.'

Wilde looked thoughtful for a moment, and then smiled. Perhaps for the first time in days. 'I see,' he said. 'By, I assume, an eighth of an inch?'

'Precisely,' Moriarty agreed.

'So this is the camera . . . '

Moriarty lifted a folded piece of foolscap from his desk. 'The camera is only recently been brought over from Bohemia, where it is manufactured,' he said. 'And only two stores in the London area have them. I have here the names of the fourteen people who have purchased a Baum-Lamphier since they first arrived six weeks ago.' He handed the paper to

Wilde. 'Do you recognize a name?'

Wilde perused the list, his finger running down the page, muttering the names to himself. Then he suddenly sat back and exclaimed a sharp epithet, which I will not record here.

'Ah!' said Moriarty. 'There is a familiar name on the list?'

'Bromire,' Wilde said, spitting the name out. 'Alexis Bromire.'

'And he is?'

'The company's lighting director.'

'I suspected as much,' Moriarty said. 'The contrast and the lack of shadow in the photograph made me suspect that the scene had been carefully — and perhaps professionally — lit.'

'A strutting little man with a repulsive toothbrush of a mustache occupying much of his upper lip,' Wilde said. 'Dresses in overly-tailored black suits like a — ' Wilde searched for a phrase ' — like a dancing mortician.'

'What do we do?' I asked. 'We can't very well go to the police.'

'I suggest we pay Mr. Bromire a visit,' Moriarty said. 'Perhaps we can convince him of the error of his rather repulsive ways.' Rising, he opened the left-hand drawer of his desk and removed a Webley service revolver, which he thrust into the pocket of his suit jacket.

'I say,' I said, 'you're not going to — '

'It is best to be prepared for any eventuality,' Moriarty said.

'It does rather ruin the, ah, hang of the jacket,' Wilde commented. 'I'd rather go unarmed into the fray than have the line of my suit compromised.'

'I have an underarm holster some-where,' Moriarty said, 'but that makes an unattractive bulge over the heart.'

'An insufficiently explored sartorial challenge,' Wilde said. 'Do you have Bromire's address?'

'I do,' said Moriarty. He lives in Notting Hill.'

'I should have guessed,' said Wilde.

It was an unattractive gray day and the snow had turned to slush when we left Moriarty's house. Mr. Maws ran to the corner and, after several blasts on his whistle, managed to secure us a four-wheeler.

It was about quarter past four when we pulled up in front of the house, an old Georgian with four Doric columns astride the front door and a round window above. It had been broken up into flats in the distant past, and Bromire occupied the first floor left front. The front door was off latch and we entered and started up a wide staircase that had probably been one of the features of the house before it had been cloven.

We heard the yelling when we reached the first landing. It came thinly through the walls, but there was no doubt that it would be a quality performance if we were in the room from which it emanated. Two voices: one shrill and the other low and growling like an angry dog. There was a staccato quality to the sounds, as though the actors were taking short breaks for air, or to dredge up new and fresh invectives before recommencing their mutual verbal abuse.

'What do you suppose — ' I began, when the remainder of my supposition was cut off by two sharp cracks and a scream. Then silence.

'Gunshots!' Moriarty exclaimed, running up the stairs ahead of us. We followed close on his heels.

Bromire's door was closed, and Moriarty knocked, waited for a second, and when he got no response slammed his foot powerfully against the lock. At the third kick the door burst open and we rushed into the room.

The scene that greeted us was like a tableau from the Grand Guignol: to our right a slim young man in his shirt sleeves, collar askew, hair scrambled, eyes wild, panting violently from fear and panic. His face and neck seemed to be covered with small scratches. He was holding a small revolver limply in his right hand, which was mottled with a curious blue stain. To our left, an overturned table, papers, photographic plates, envelopes and writing materials scattered about the floor. And, behind it, the crumpled body of a small, immaculately-dressed man lying in an ever-widening pool of his own blood.

The young man started away from us in a panic but stopped as a look of recognition crossed his face. 'Mr. Wilde,' he exclaimed. 'Is it you? Ah, I see that it is. I'm glad that you've come. But how did you — ' he broke off and stared down at the body. 'But never mind. It's too late — too late!'

'Reynard!' Wilde said. 'What are you doing here?'

'The same as you, I fancy,' the young man said. 'Trying to come to terms with a blackmailer.'

'Unsuccessfully, I gather,' Moriarty said.

'He came at me and — ' Reynard shook his head. 'But who are you?'

'My name is Professor Moriarty. I've come to assist Mr. Wilde in resolving this, ah, matter.'

'What on earth happened here?' Wilde asked.

'Let us come inside and close the door,' Moriarty suggested. 'There doesn't seem to be anyone else in the building — or at least on this floor — now, or someone would assuredly have appeared in the hall. But people should be coming home from their day's work any time now, and we don't want to attract unnecessary attention.'

We entered the flat and closed the door behind us as best we could. Most of the door was still in place, but the lock had burst out from the last kick. 'What other rooms are there?' Moriarty asked.

'There's a bedroom and a lav, and a sort of kitchen — the sort that isn't much good for actually cooking,' Reynard said.

Moriarty nodded. 'Now,' he said. 'What are you doing here?'

'Are you going to call the police?' Reynard asked, keeping has voice steady.

'Should we?' Moriarty responded.

'Needless to say, I'd prefer it if you didn't,' said Reynard. 'He was a vile blackmailer, and he's better off dead, don't you think?'

'There is a law against killing people,' Wilde commented. 'Even blackmailers and wealthy maiden aunts.'

We turned to look at Wilde, who shrugged. 'It just came out that way,' he explained. 'When I begin a sentence it often wanders off in unexpected directions. That, I fancy, is my genius.'

'In this case,' I said, 'if there was any way — surely Moriarty, there must be some way . . . '

'I think I should thank you, Reynard,' Wilde said, 'and then perhaps we should all get out of here and let the police make what they will of this. Does anyone know you're here?'

'Only you gentlemen,' Reynard answered.

Moriarty shook his head slowly 'I think perhaps we had better call the police after all,' he said.

I looked at him in surprise. 'You? Of all people, you?'

'It's one thing to cover up for a man who has just rid the world of a blackmailer,' Moriarty said deliberately. 'It's quite another to help his accomplice escape justice.'

'What?' Wilde exclaimed. 'But why do you think — '

'I'm sure of it,' Moriarty said. 'Look at his hand.'

'His hand?'

'That blue stain. It's from the developing solution. Mr. Reynard has been developing the plates. He is not a victim. He is an accomplice. It took two people to do this — to carry you downstairs and set you up for the scene, if nothing else.'

'Well, I'll — ' Wilde began. 'Reynard, why would you . . . '

Reynard raised the pistol and held it rock-steady in his hand, pointing at Moriarty. He pulled back the hammer. 'All right, Professor Whatever-Your-Name-Is. Think you're smart, do you? Well I'm — '

That was as far as he got. One shot from Moriarty's Webley, fired from in the coat pocket, tore into his chest and he was dead before he hit the ground.

There was a moment of shocked silence, and then Wilde said, 'I'll be — I don't know what I'll be.'

'Unfortunate, but perhaps it's better this way. You'd never have been free of him if he got away,' Moriarty told Wilde. 'Search the flat for photographic plates, while I arrange the bodies to make it look like mutual destruction. Then we'd best cautiously leave the scene.'

'He was not a gentleman,' Wilde said

decisively. 'One can tell by the cravat. A true gentleman has an unerring taste in cravats.'

'And we'd best take the camera, too,' Moriarty said.

And so we left. None of us, to my knowledge, ever spoke of the incident again.

THE END

We do hope that you have enjoyed reading this large print book.

Did you know that all of our titles are available for purchase?

We publish a wide range of high quality large print books including:
**Romances, Mysteries, Classics
General Fiction
Non Fiction and Westerns**

Special interest titles available in large print are:
**The Little Oxford Dictionary
Music Book, Song Book
Hymn Book, Service Book**

Also available from us courtesy of Oxford University Press:
**Young Readers' Dictionary
(large print edition)
Young Readers' Thesaurus
(large print edition)**

For further information or a free brochure, please contact us at:
**Ulverscroft Large Print Books Ltd.,
The Green, Bradgate Road, Anstey,
Leicester, LE7 7FU, England.
Tel:** (00 44) 0116 236 4325
Fax: (00 44) 0116 234 0205

ONE WAY OUT

John Russell Fearn
& Philip Harbottle

London financier Morgan Dale is travelling by train to Scotland with his chief clerk, Martin Lee. Suddenly he's confronted by the woman who'd been obsessed by him — his ex-secretary Janice Elton. Dale had recently sacked her and spurned her romantic advances, but now she wants revenge. However, when Lee returns to their carriage, he finds Janice's dead body and Dale claiming she'd committed suicide by taking strychnine. Soon there will be only one way out for Dale . . .

THE MAN IN THE DARK

Donald Stuart

In Burma, the British manager of the ruby mines of Mogok has been away, attempting to track down a leopard that had been attacking livestock. He returns to discover his stand-in at the office lying dead on the floor, the safe door open and its contents stolen. Fifty of the mine's finest rubies had been awaiting shipment to the company's London office. Those jewels, seemingly endowed with evil powers, are destined to cause numerous men to meet their deaths . . .

DEADLY PURSUIT

Steve Hayes & Andrea Wilson

When New York businesswoman Jackie O'Hara finds out that she's terminally ill, she must put her affairs in order, and top of her list is making peace with her estranged brother Danny. But Danny, sole witness to a high-profile gangland murder, is on the run from the Russian Mafia. Jackie begins her worldwide search for Danny knowing she's in a race against time. However, she could surprise everyone and live for years — or she might die today, or tomorrow.

ENEMY OF THE STATE

E. C. Tubb

Security Services in the West are jittery with the renewal of the Cold War. Civilization has grown complex and vulnerable to an internal enemy. An act of sabotage could be unleashed on a massive scale — an atom bomb can be carried in a suitcase . . . This nightmare is realised when an enemy agent plants an atom bomb, set to detonate imminently. It must be located and deactivated, before thousands die and an entire town becomes radioactive ash . . .